I0726190

CHRISTINE A. SCHIMPF

Falling for Chet

Christine A. Schimpf

Faith Statement

Romans 8:28 And we know that for those who love God all things work together for good, for those who are called according to his purpose (ESV)

Chapter One

Chet Taylor strode up the concrete stairs of the church two at a time. He was planning to grab the first available seat once he was inside, but he detected a pair of pretty velvet heels and the woman who wore them standing next to him. It was hard not to notice her with her jet-black hair and the white woolen coat that cinched at the waist. It was a striking combination. He opened the door and then stepped aside. "I beg your pardon, after you. Friends of the groom or the bride?" he asked, hoping to discover more about the beauty before she disappeared into the chapel.

Her dark hair swayed with a flutter of wind, moving a scent of lilac in Chet's direction. Her almond-shaped face and full lips gave way to a petite frame, and the look she gave him with her blue-violet eyes radiated confidence. To say she was gorgeous would have been an understatement. Chet stood there, frozen in time, and waited for her response.

The smile she gave him broke the ice between them. "The bride. I'm Andrea Lockhart." A soft thank you fell from her berry-colored lips, and she slipped inside the church.

Chet intended to follow her, hoping for the opportunity she hadn't given him to introduce himself. But it took a minute for his eyes to adjust to the interior's dim lighting, losing sight of her entirely. So instead, he squeezed into one of the last seats in the back of the church and waited for his friend Conrad Hamilton's wedding to begin.

~

Andrea Lockhart couldn't believe her bad luck as she walked down the aisle on the arm of one of the ushers. Not only had she just made it in time for the wedding of her dear friend, Lila Clark, but now she was being led to the front of the church, drawing much-unwanted attention. She hadn't even given the handsome stranger who'd opened the door for her an opportunity to introduce himself.

Now seated on a wooden pew near the front of the church, Andrea noticed the elegant touches throughout the chapel. Creamy white satin bows, white and red roses, and soft light glowing from wall sconces. With gentle snow falling outside, it appeared the New Year's Eve wedding of the year was happening right here in this beautiful stone church in the Door County countryside. Andrea shushed the memories from her own marriage that ended in shambles. She didn't want to clutter this perfect day with all the reasons why she was still single. Her mother did a good job reminding her of that.

Andrea shifted her thoughts to the literary conference where she'd met Lila. While she was scouting for new clients, Lila was in search of an agent for her first series. After signing Lila, the two women became colleagues and soon good friends. Two professional, single women living in New York and pursuing their careers acted as the glue between them. Lila's career had quickly taken off, and she was an established author, but Andrea found herself once again at a crossroads in her career because of a merger at the agency. Now she was without a job, and all she had left to work with was hope for a brand-new start in life.

"Andrea?" Cassie Hamilton stood nearby, interrupting her thoughts. She wore a red velvet gown and the tiniest baby's breath woven into a waterfall braid that fell past her shoulders. The groom's sister was a Christmas vision. Andrea gave her a warm smile, happy to see her.

"I'm so glad you made it. How was your flight out of LaGuardia with all that snow?"

Andrea rolled her eyes. "We sat on the tarmac for an hour de-icing, but I made it. Wouldn't have missed it. It's good to see you."

"Let's catch up after the service. I'll find you." Cassie waved a hand and then walked toward the back of the church.

The soft music of violins swept through the chapel. The matron of honor started her walk down the aisle wearing the palest shade of red. Like Cassie's style, her long, dark tendrils cascaded down her back. Andrea searched the wedding booklet for her name. *Matron of Honor, Mrs. Melanie Winters.* So, this was Lila's childhood best friend. Like every detail about the wedding so far, Mrs. Winters fit the part beautifully.

~

Chet scanned the area for the pretty woman he'd met at the doorstep. Instead, he met the eyes of Olivia Hawkins, the woman he'd recently stopped dating. She threw him a warm smile. Chet responded with a nod. It would've been easy to have her on his arm today.

The music changed, lassoing Chet's thoughts. He watched Melanie Winters walk down the aisle when a rainbow of sparkles caught his attention. At first, he assumed it was a unique lighting effect, but he traced the flickering to one of the guests. The pretty woman he met at the door. Andrea Lockhart. He craned his neck to better the view, rubbing shoulders with the man seated next to him. He mouthed a sorry, but his attention soon returned to Andrea. She wore a simple grey-toned gown with a row of gemstones around the neckline that caught the light at the slightest movement. She stood out among the crowd like a ripened apple from one of their trees on the farm. *She's not from around here.*

His smartphone buzzed in his pocket, pulling him out of his trance-like state. Why hadn't he shut it off? He hoped it wasn't the bank calling to remind him of the overdue payment again. Irritated, he retrieved his phone and glanced at the incoming call. *Dad.* They'd talked over lunch about a few issues regarding the farm, but his dad was aware of his plans to attend the wedding. He wouldn't call unless it was critical. Chet stifled a groan. The last thing he needed was another argument, but if they didn't see eye-to-eye soon, the whole farm would go up in financial smoke.

Violin music eased Chet's shoulders and upper back. Earlier today, he'd helped the construction crew install metal shelving units in the last of the new greenhouses. The day's work left his shoulders sore and a good-sized bruise on his upper back for not seeing one of the support beams soon enough. Ignoring the pain, Chet craned his neck to get a glimpse of the woman he spotted before he was interrupted, but when the congregation stood as Lila entered the room, it made his attempt impossible. He followed the eyes of those around him and soon found out why everyone appeared so transfixed. He'd never seen Lila as beautiful as she was right now.

Conrad's bride walked past him. Her eyes were on her groom. The silky fabric of her gown reminded him of fresh cream. Chet sighed. Conrad was a lucky man. He noticed a little flower girl tossing rose petals on the white runner and a little boy carrying the rings on a satin pillow with a death-like grip. *I can see my kids doing that one day.* The sight was adorable.

His gaze moved to Conrad, who stood next to his brother and best man, Luke. The two men dressed in dark suits stood like two recruits after being sworn into service. Their postures were solid and erect. One of them, with clear eyes for the future that waited for him. The other with unwavering support. Even from this distance, Chet envied what he saw. The unmistakable expression of love. It was written all over Conrad's face.

He remembered Conrad and Lila's story of how they went their separate ways, but both believed God had used their circumstances to bring them back together and fall in love all over again. If only he hadn't made so many mistakes, maybe God would have brought someone special into *his* life. A partner all of his own. In his weakest moments, Chet feared he'd never find her.

Chapter Two

After the service, Andrea inched her way through the receiving line, watching Lila accept congratulatory kisses and Conrad firm handshakes. Like a pair of seasoned dancers, the couple already seemed to move in sync with each other. Andrea exhaled a sigh of sheer happiness for her friend. In all the years she'd known Lila, Andrea had never seen her radiate like she did today. A contentment Andrea had never seen before was written all over her face because of the love she'd found with this man. Andrea remembered that feeling with her first husband, Ben.

When Andrea's eyes met Lila's, they shared a nostalgic smile, each realizing a chapter in their lives would end. Their friendship would change and be challenged in the miles between New York and Wisconsin. Yet, despite the thrill Lila must be feeling right now, Andrea's heart gave a selfish tug. Would she ever know this happiness again?

Andrea stepped into Lila's arms, returning a friendly hug. "You're a gorgeous bride. I've missed you these last few months, and now you're never coming back. How do you expect me to manage my life without my best friend?" she teased. "I need your help to find a new job."

Lila nodded. "You'll find something quicker than you think. You're good at what you do. I'm sure Jim is working on it even now while you're away."

Andrea nodded. "He is. If he hadn't promised my dad to watch over my career, I'm not sure where I would've ended up, but enough about me. I'm anxious to meet your knight in shining armor."

Lila placed a light hand across Conrad's shoulder, immediately redirecting his attention to her. "Conrad, I'd like you to meet Andrea Lockhart, my agent for many years and a dear friend. She spent many tireless hours steering my writing career into the hands of the right publishers."

The tall man at Lila's side turned toward Andrea. His shoulders, broad and robust, reminded her of the statue of a lumberjack near a pancake house she'd passed when entering the village. His eyes, the warm color of espresso, crinkled at the corners as he smiled at her. Andrea knew at once she liked him.

"Don't hate me too much for stealing your best friend," Conrad said.

What a wonderful sense of humor. Andrea gave the groom a warm smile and extended her hand. "I can see how easily that could have happened just by looking at you. Congratulations to you both."

Conrad bypassed a handshake and pulled Andrea into his arms in a firm hug. "Thank you, Andrea," Conrad replied, "I hope we have a chance to get to know each other while you're here."

"I look forward to it," she said.

"Now go find yourself a handsome stranger to talk to. There's plenty here." Lila said, but Andrea rolled her eyes with that task. *Fat chance.* If there was anyone unlucky in love, it was her.

She followed the other guests into a small gathering place intended for the guests. The scent of brewed coffee filled the air. As if part of the arrangements, gentle snow continued to fall outside, adding another layer of coziness to the room and excitement for the night ahead. Everything seemed to be falling into place, and Andrea was getting swept up in all of it.

She drifted toward the coffee station admiring the Christmas colors in the decorations. She wasn't one to believe in predictions but felt that something marvelous was about to happen. She lifted a mug of hot cocoa from the tray and smiled down at the marshmallow cream sprinkled with specks of red sugar when a man's voice behind her interrupted her first sip.

"I hope you don't mind the intrusion, but what would you recommend?"

Andrea's shoulders stiffened. Why did men feel they could hook-up at a wedding? Especially with her – a divorced woman with absolutely no interest or time to get involved? She wanted to tell him to move on but then remembered Lila's advice. She had to start somewhere, or she'd end up alone. Jobless and alone, forever. She turned to find a striking man smiling down at her. He looked as if he belonged on a beach somewhere, not on the snowy landscapes of Wisconsin, with his sun-bleached hair and eyes the color of the Caribbean Sea. Then she recognized him. *It's the handsome stranger at the door.* "Since I don't know you, I have no idea."

The jet-black suit he wore strained across his broad shoulders as he moved. His Christmas red button-down shirt and skinny grey tie worked beautifully to complement his looks. A strong back, muscular legs, and large hands eluded a physical work line.

The only thing missing was a cowboy hat when he tipped his head. He had a rare, rustic appeal that she was willing to wager he used to his advantage. His lips parted to share a smile that would make most women weak in the knees, but Andrea knew better than to give too much merit to the power of an attractive man. Ben was also good-looking, which was now a bit of a red flag for Andrea.

"Can we start over?" he asked. "I'm Chet Taylor, a business acquaintance of Conrad's. He's a fine carpenter. He's done a good amount of work for our family farm." He offered her his hand.

She felt the calluses and the strength in his grip and doubted he had a standing appointment with a manicurist like most men she knew back in New York.

"Andrea Lockhart," they said together.

"We met at the door," he said.

Andrea nodded. "Yes, I'm … was Lila's literary agent."

"Conrad mentioned Lila's agent, but he left out some more important details."

Did he give her the once over? Andrea fumed. "I'm not sure I believe that, but it was very nice to meet you, Mr. Taylor." Andrea slipped her hand from his grasp, not believing Conrad had mentioned a word to him. Now she could tell Lila she'd talked with a man and an attractive one. Big step.

Chet appeared amused with her retort. The look on his face told her he wasn't used to being shrugged off, but the last thing she was prepared for was what came next – a boisterous laugh that rang in her ears. She scanned the room, looking for others who shared her opinion, but no one else seemed to notice.

"You're an intriguing woman, Andrea Lockhart. Would you do me the honor of saving me the first dance?"

Was it flattery or embarrassment that prevented her from answering? *The honor?* She lifted her chin to meet his gaze, but before she could refuse him, the clang of a handbell rang loud in the room.

"If I could have your attention, please, my name is Cassie Hamilton. For those of you who may not know me, I'm the groom's sister, and it's my job to tell you it's time to start the reception at Window Shopping."

A round of applause broke out among the crowd, followed by quickened steps to the coat check. Andrea was swept into the hallway with the others, leaving Chet behind her without an answer to his question. She didn't intend on staying long after the dinner. Watching other couples swaying to the music on the dance floor wouldn't help her melancholy state of mind toward love.

She slipped on her coat and inched her fingers into her gloves. What kind of dance would he have selected for us? Stepping outside, she lifted the collar of her coat to protect her face from the cold, but not before glancing back into the room. Chet's eyes locked in on hers. If she had to guess, he looked more like a waltz type of man, and lucky for her, that was her father's favorite dance. Not that it mattered, of course.

Chapter 3

Andrea set the wipers on high to clear the windshield and then drove her car to the reception. Plunging her feet into the snow-covered road, she ignored the powerful protest from her feet and wished for a warm pair of fur-lined boots. Using a herculean effort, she navigated across the street and kept her sights on the entry door of Window Shopping. How did Melanie Winters turn her ordinary gift shop into a wedding hall? This she had to see.

The music of violins greeted her at the door. She handed her coat to the attendant, who threw her an exuberant smile. After smoothing away nonexistent wrinkles from her dress, her eyes caught the dark wet spots on her black velvet shoes. She wrinkled her nose in disappointment.

"You'll find the seat assignment table straight ahead," the attendant told her.

Andrea thanked the young man and then strolled into the gathering space welcoming the warmth in the room. Ambient light peeked through the looped Christmas-red paper streamers. Oversized papier-mache balls swung freely above, adding a flair of festivity. Even the thick icicles hanging outside added to the magical feel inside this room. Crisp winter white linens covered round tables of eight in the dining area. English lace dinnerware gleamed with polished platinum edges. *Did I wander into a fairy tale?* Closing her eyes, she breathed in the exquisite scent of evergreen and roses, loving the fragrance of Christmas.

Her pleasant thoughts were interrupted by rowdy laughter from across the room. Her ears led her eyes to Chet. He stood in the center of attention among a group of friends, including a few attractive women. She wasn't surprised. He flashed her a wide grin, which she ignored. The last thing Chet Taylor needed was encouragement, especially from her.

A young waiter approached. "May I suggest a glass of champagne or sparkling water?" He presented the tray to her as if she'd already answered yes to his question. The fluted glasses and bubbly beverages looked appealing. Why not?

"I believe I will. Thank you." She sipped the amber liquid, and despite herself, she couldn't help but watch the man who'd introduced himself to her earlier. Chet moved from one guest to another, shaking hands or giving a playful elbow jab in the ribs to those around him. From the looks of it, he was well-liked.

Does he realize how lucky he is to have the gift of so many friendships? Envy festered somewhere deep inside of her. Her drive to stay competitive in her field kept her busy to have little time for anything else but work. Even her personal time had a work-related focus taking her social life down to a whopping zero. She knew that she'd find herself alone if she kept up this demanding pace. Forever.

Cassie strode toward her with a wide smile. "It's wonderful to see you again, Andrea."

Andrea whirled her thoughts from the man who stole her attention to the groom's sister. "I was hoping we'd have a chance to talk. You're as pretty as the bride."

Cassie's laughter filled the space between them. The resemblance between her and the groom was subtle, but the same soft brown eyes as her brother's met hers.

"Oh, I doubt that but thank you for the nice compliment. Were you as impressed as I was with the ceremony?"

Andrea's eyes widened. "Absolutely. It was simple and elegant at the same time. And Lila is beyond stunning. I'm at a loss for words even though I'm a literary agent and work with authors daily."

Cassie lowered her head. "I noticed you met Chet. He's one of a kind, isn't he?" The lift in Cassie's voice told Andrea her earlier impressions were correct.

"All the man needs is a cowboy hat." Andrea's comment caused a chuckle from both women. Her lips felt the coolness from her drink, but her eyes caught Chet's attention.

As if he'd heard his name mentioned, he lifted his head above the crowd. Then he made the most unexpected gesture. He winked at her.

Andrea squeezed the stem of the glass in her hand. Am I supposed to wink back? Uncertain how to respond to the man, Andrea was happy to follow Cassie, who steered them toward a high-top table in the other direction.

"Conrad worked a couple of jobs at Taylor Farms and said it's an impressive place. He told me Chet's one hundred percent committed since coming home last year."

"Sounds like you may be interested in this one-of-a-kind man." If that was true, Andrea wanted to know.

Across the table, Cassie laid a light hand on her chest. "Chet and I are good friends. And as far as my Prince Charming is concerned, I fear a long life as an old-fashioned spinster with a brother like Conrad. I've been told I'm not the best judge of character when it comes to men, so Conrad's decided on his own to navigate my love life. It's nothing short of embarrassing."

Andrea laughed along but doubted Cassie minded at all. She certainly wouldn't have and wished for an older brother to guide her over the years. But, at least she had Jim, a trusted colleague of her father who stepped in to oversee her career since her father's retirement from the industry. "Where did Chet come home from?" Andrea asked, convincing herself she was making polite conversation and nothing more.

Cassie shrugged, implying she didn't know the whole story. "He spent some time in Vegas but decided to come home. He's pretty set on making things right with his father. At least that's what Conrad's told me."

Andrea nodded. What was it about Chet Taylor that had her curious? And what did he have to make right with his dad? Although she'd love the answers to those questions, Andrea decided to change the subject. "Whatever happened to your plans? You wanted to start a business, right?"

Cassie's eyes widened. "You remembered? That was more than a year ago when we had that conversation," she said, referring to the one-time visit she'd made to New York.

"Your enthusiasm was over-the-top. What helped you come to a decision?"

"Since our little village is a tourist destination in

Wisconsin, we are inundated with visitors all year long, but not enough places to eat and not one bookstore."

There was a time Andrea dreamt of owning a bookstore with pretty jacketed books and inviting spaces allowing patrons the luxury of picking the right book to take home.

Cassie continued, pulling Andrea back to the conversation. "So, I closed my eyes and picked. I'm now the proud owner of an adorable café with a small breakfast menu and various coffee blends."

Andrea nodded. "Smart move, especially with no competition. Who doesn't like a strong cup of java at any point in the day? I'm a coffeeholic myself," Andrea whispered as if drinking too much coffee was something to hide.

Cassie chuckled. "The smell of roasting coffee brings back fond memories for me. My parents started every morning with a fresh-brewed pot. They both had busy lives, but that was the one habit they never gave up. Sharing coffee first thing every morning."

"Some of the best novels I've read start with an opening scene like that one. It sounds like you're on track."

"I can't think of a better way to start a day," Cassie beamed.

Andrea smiled, admiring the clear vision ahead of the young entrepreneur and the murky one ahead of her. When were the chips going to fall in her direction? Ever? She divorced four years ago, and now she lost her job.

"I have a concern, though."

Cassie's remark pulled Andrea out of the doldrums. She stole a sip from her glass. She didn't expect a problem to emerge. Cassie appeared to have everything in order. "What's that?"

"I'm curious as to who will rent the building next door."

Andrea nodded. The wrong kind of business might do more harm than good. Cassie had a point.

"In the end, it's all in God's hands. Worry for nothing as scripture tells us, right?" Cassie asked.

Andrea smiled. If only she could agree with that train of thought as she once had. So much had changed.

"How are things going at the agency?" Cassie asked.

Andrea shrugged. "Messy. A merger left me without a job. So, I've started a new job search."

Cassie frowned. "Sometimes change is good."

Andrea didn't want to delve into her job search plans. Cassie's life sounded much more enjoyable at this point. "Maybe. I'm sure I'll find something in the end. What's next on your list?"

"My first order of business is getting ready for opening day and then finding marketing opportunities. No one will come if they don't know I exist."

"Maybe I can help with the marketing. I read a fascinating article about the lavender on Washington Island on my flight over. Is that something you'd consider offering in the café? Even on a small scale? It may attract another demographic."

"I never thought of that, but it's worth exploring. And maybe the lavender farm would offer my coffee blends?"

"I'm inhaling a premium roasted coffee in one breath and lavender in another. It works for me." Andrea was sure she'd be one of Cassie's regular customers if she lived in the area. A fan of both coffee and the calming scent of lavender seemed like a good fit to her.

Cassie laid a light hand on Andrea's shoulder. "Now that's the brainstorming ideas I could use. Would you consider going into business with me?"

Even though Andrea knew Cassie was joking, she played along and raised her hands against the idea. "Believe me. I have my hands full, especially if I want to break into something new."

"Will you come down and see the café before you leave? I'm right on Bay Street."

Andrea recalled Cassie's brief visit to New York last year. She found her to be an insightful woman and a good listener. She was confident she'd be one of those rare successes in life simply because of who she was. "I'd love to. Isn't Bay Street in the hub of the downtown area?"

"It is. With enough prayers and persistence, dreams do come true."

"I agree. Prayer is a powerful resource." The words fell so quickly from her lips, but like reading her Bible, Andrea seldom shared conversations with God anymore. Growing up, she was a regular chatterbox in her alone time with Him. But despite her pleading and prayers, He'd let her first marriage fail. When the divorce decree arrived in the mail, Andrea decided to focus on the tangibles in life, like her career. She was a living example of how prayer didn't always work things out for good.

Cassie scanned the room. "Looks like we'd better find our seats. Don't forget to come to visit me before you leave."

"I will." Andrea returned the smile, finding that rare camaraderie with a new friend.

Chapter Four

Chet thumped Conrad on the back. The groom whirled around with a broad smile as if he'd just heard the punchline of a great joke. Wow, Chet thought, he looks like he won the lottery.

Conrad grabbed Chet's hand in a fierce handshake. "Chet, it's good to see you. I spotted you earlier in church, but I was afraid you'd left."

"Nah, I just had to call Dad before sitting down for dinner. I want to congratulate you on taking the plunge. Thanks a lot for decreasing our numbers." Chet couldn't deny the look of joy on his friend's face. A twinge of jealousy stirred in his gut.

Conrad roared with laughter. "By one? You might be on the run now, buddy, but I heard your days are numbered. Aren't you dating an attorney from Sturgeon Bay?"

Chet spotted Olivia across the room laughing at someone's joke. She looked nice today. "It didn't work out. I'm still free and clear."

"Uh-huh." Conrad navigated them to a high-top table out of earshot of the others. He signaled one of the waiters for a fresh round of drinks. "Hey, how's it going at the farm?"

Chet cringed and then drained his glass. He wished Conrad hadn't brought up the topic. He was trying not to think about the debt hanging over the farm's head. The last issue he wanted to discuss was how things were *not* going well with his dad. "Hanging in, that's about it. I'm counting on a fresh revenue stream from the B&B."

Conrad nodded, agreeing with the idea. "Speak to your dad about going organic yet?"

Chet shook his head. *Here it comes.*

"Why not, man? The last time we had talked, the move seemed like a no-brainer." He shot Chet a surprised look.

Chet scanned the room as if bored. "Can't seem to find the right time to bring it up. I won't push him. It causes more arguments than its worth."

Conrad replied with a pensive look. "If I remember right, you did the research. Don't wait too long to talk to him. Dreams have a way of dying, and then you're just working a job."

Conrad hit the nail on the head. Lately, that's how it felt, but Chet was pinned between his vision for the business and keeping his dad happy. He knew coming back to the farm meant making up for old mistakes. That would take time – a commodity Chet didn't have. Not with the bank crawling down their throats.

Conrad tipped his glass to his lips. His gaze zeroed in on Chet. "You know the old man forgave you for all the mistakes you think you've made."

Chet wasn't expecting Conrad to remember the details of his past. Last year, they'd had a few conversations when Conrad and his crew were out at the farm building the greenhouses. Chet hadn't meant to share as much as he had but it was easy talking with

Conrad. He didn't cast judgment either, which would've been easy against a guy who took off leaving the family business behind him. Instead, Conrad talked about everything happening for a reason and all being part of God's plan. It had opened Chet's eyes to a truth he'd long forgotten.

"Yeah, maybe."

"You're a visionary. Don't waste that gift."

Chet grunted. "Right." Although he and Conrad had talked last year, he omitted a part of the truth – the fact it was a miracle he had come back to the farm. He'd only darkened the doorway because his brother put the screws to him after their father's stroke. Chet would never have had the courage to show his face back home again if it hadn't been for Chuck. Moving to Vegas to pursue the life of a card shark had left him nothing to show for it. "I appreciate the advice, but if I'm not mistaken, I witnessed another brave soul stepping off the cliff this afternoon in that chapel down the street. So, we're here to celebrate, right?"

"Damn straight we are," Conrad said.

Even though the situation at the farm was serious, Chet was pleased the topic was closed. He grinned as he watched his friend slip back into the shoes of a newly married man.

Chapter Five

After locating her seat assignment, Andrea drifted into the dining area. She ran her finger down the satin tablecloths and picked up the aroma of freshly baked bread that filled the room. She closed her eyes. The delicious smell reminded her of home.

"Take a guess why the reception is here."

Startled, Andrea didn't hear the man approach but recognized his voice in her next breath. *Chet.* She turned to face him, noticing the broad smile when her attention was all his. The handsome stranger standing in front of her had her tongue-tied for a split second.

Thankful he couldn't read her body language, she tucked a strand of loose hair behind her right ear.

Chet's hand enveloped hers, making it feel small. "Don't do that."

Andrea blinked. His comment came with an air of authority. "Do what?"

"Put your hair back. It was nice just as it was, sassy and out of place."

Andrea didn't give his comment a second

thought. Instead, she steered the conversation in a different direction. "You were about to explain why the reception is here at Window Shopping."

He gestured across the room. "This is where Lila and Conrad ran into each other after years of being apart. When Melanie brought that to their attention, the decision to have the reception here was easy."

Andrea followed Chet's gaze to the back of the room near a rear exit. "That sounds like either the start or the end of a good book," she said.

"I'm being honest here." Chet raised an eyebrow reminding Andrea of her favorite cousin. The gesture caused a smile to slip from Andrea's lips.

"If that's true, it's a lovely beginning to a beautiful end. The ceremony was touching. I can't wait to see what the evening holds." Andrea twirled the empty fluted glass in her hand while Chet signaled for a waiter.

Lila may have mentioned Chet to her in their phone conversations, but the image Andrea created in her mind didn't match the interesting man standing before her now.

"I'm surprised we haven't met until today, having known both Conrad and Lila. First visit to Door County?" he asked.

"It is, but I can tell you from what I've seen on my drive up here, it reminds me of Buffalo."

Chet moved closer allowing Andrea a closer look at his strong chin, broad nose, and gorgeous eyes. "Is that home?"

Andrea found herself swimming through the scent of his leather-scented cologne. She nodded in answer to his question. "Born and raised."

"Good memories, I hope."

Andrea grinned, remembering her past. "The best. Especially the summers. I used to visit my cousin's farm. I can still see the kitchen table filled with my Aunt Linda's fresh blueberry waffles." Andrea closed her eyes, revisiting the memory. When she opened them, she found Chet studying her face setting off the butterflies in her stomach.

"This may surprise you, but my mother's from upstate New York, and she loves reminding us of it too."

"What do you mean?"

The look in his eyes was reminiscent of good times. "All the memories we heard about and all the trips we took to visit family. I can almost taste the Adirondack soda." He handed her a fresh glass of bubbly from the tray.

"So much like root beer." Andrea placed the emptied glass on the tray and accepted the refreshed one from Chet.

His eyes widened. "You've had it?"

She could hear the surprise in his question. "I have," she nodded, sending her hair askew but not putting it back into place this time.

"Black and whites?" He shot her a doubtful look, revealing the face of a much younger version of himself.

"The little cookies with vanilla and chocolate icing?" Andrea fought a giggle. "You're making me hungry. I love them. How did your family end up here? Wisconsin is a long way from New York."

"My dad had an opportunity to have a business all his own. He left a stellar career in sales and bought the farm. He moved us cross-country and never looked back. He'll tell you he has no regrets."

"Impressive. Your father sounds like an authentic entrepreneur."

Chet nodded, and Andrea thought she saw something flash over his eyes. Loss? Pain?

"That he is," Chet said with absolute certainty.

"That's a path I had hoped to walk down myself one day, but now I'm unsure." Andrea was surprised she shared such a personal piece of her life with this man, an almost total stranger to her.

A set of lines crossed over Chet's brow. "Oh?" He removed his suit jacket and rolled up the sleeves of his shirt.

"A merger at the agency has left me without a job."

Chet blew out a response. "That's tough."

Andrea nodded, uncertain how she'd process the impending changes. She almost wished she hadn't mentioned the topic, but it was easy talking with him. "Something will come up. It always does."

Chet smiled, "Are you still living in Buffalo?"

Andrea smiled. "Manhattan, which is quite a funny set of circumstances. I won my apartment on a bet with Lila, but that's a long story."

Chet let out a whistle, taking Andrea by surprise, especially in a formal setting. She scanned the room, but the other guests seemed oblivious to the gesture.

"You must be pretty resourceful if you managed to win an apartment on a bet."

Andrea shrugged a shoulder. "I never thought I'd win. Marketing authors and negotiating contracts are what I do for a living, so I'm used to betting on the odds."

Chet could relate. "Are you any good at it?"

She gaped at him. *Is he serious?* "I beg your pardon?"

He raised a hand, stopping her. "Hold on, hold on. I used to bet on the odds too. I was asking the question because I'm looking for advice."

Andrea frowned. He certainly was a man of few filters. She was curious about how often he was misunderstood with such an unorthodox style. "I've had success and failures like most of my colleagues. What's the issue, if you don't mind me asking?" She placed her glass on a nearby high-top table and gave him her full attention. Despite the free and easy way he'd presented himself, she sensed he was troubled, allowing her to connect the dots from a moment ago.

"My dad and I run Taylor Farms. We supply the county with fresh produce."

Andrea's eyes widened. "The entire county? That's impressive." She remembered her summer visits to her Aunt Linda and her large garden. Occasionally, her aunt would ask her to pull a few onions or a ripe tomato for dinner, but commercial gardening was out of her realm.

Chet's eyes sparkled as he talked about sinking his hands into the dirt and growing something extraordinary from a tiny seed. His enthusiasm for his work was hard to miss. Andrea found it both refreshing and puzzling. What on earth could be the problem?

"I don't want to overwhelm you with too many details, but we've streamlined our produce to align with demand. And we've learned a lot along the way, like what to keep and what doesn't sell. For instance, eggplant."

Andrea wiggled her nose in distaste. She tried it once and never gave it a second chance. "Eggplant?" she squeaked.

He chuckled. "Your response is pretty typical. Unfortunately, it doesn't move, so we cut it from our offerings."

"It sounds like you know what you're doing. What's going on?"

Chet exhaled. "Aww, I don't want to bore you."

Is he kidding? Andrea was fascinated. "No, please, I'd love to hear about it. You said yourself I might be able to help."

Chet leaned an elbow on the high-top table, drawing his chiseled features closer to her. My goodness, he was beautiful.

"It's pretty simple. We have a small line of organics that sell well, and I want to capitalize on that and go a hundred percent organic. But unfortunately, my father wants to keep things just as they are, and I want to broaden the business into brand-new avenues. I'm sure you've heard the story before. So, we're stuck, and the clock is ticking. The bank would like its payments and we're a little behind. Revenue is stronger with the organic line."

Andrea nodded, doing her best to keep from admiring the muscles tense in Chet's arms. Andrea studied him for a moment. This entire conversation had taken her by surprise. She assumed Chet Taylor was nothing more than a fanciful flirt. This side of him proved how wrong first impressions could be. "Here's some advice from someone who understands very little about farming but quite a bit about people. Do you want to hear it?"

His look was instantaneous, somewhere between a question and a smile. It was adorable and threw Andrea entirely off her guard and the point she wanted to make.

"I asked for it, so I'm all ears," he said with a wide grin.

Andrea managed a smile. Her idea of offering advice seemed to amuse him, and she liked him amused. His strong sense of humor reminded her of her father, who often had his family in tears. "Business strategies work across the board for most industries. It sounds like you're trying to sell an idea to your father. From what I know about book sales, at least from selling an author's work to a publishing house, it begins with active listening skills. You also need to keep your ears open to your father's hot-button topics and pain points."

"I'm sure I can figure out the hot buttons, but pain points?" Chet shook his head. "I'm not familiar with the term."

"The frustrating elements of the business. All the issues you avoid talking about because of the friction it causes between you and your dad. If you can solve some of those issues with an organic solution, you'll have better odds moving the company toward what you envision as its future."

He took a step back and then cleared his throat. "Ms. Lockhart, not only can you win an apartment on a bet, but you also managed to knock my socks off tonight with some good advice. I'm impressed."

Andrea rolled her eyes. She couldn't remember the last time she'd heard that phrase.

Chet inched toward her when the lights dimmed, signaling the guests to take their seats for dinner. "Where are you seated?" he asked.

There it was again, the scent of his cologne, was it leather or coffee? It hit her like the splash of a wave. She rubbed away the army of goosebumps running up her arms. Was there an open door somewhere allowing a blast of cold air into the room? She searched her surroundings but found nothing amiss. Was Lila right? Had it really been a year since her last date? "Table eight," she answered him, almost hoping he was on the other side of the room. She needed to get a hold of herself and sitting near him wouldn't help.

"Well, I consider this a privilege or just plain

good luck."

Andrea's breath caught. She knew the answer to the question but asked it anyway. "What do you mean?"

His response came as quick as the flickering lights overhead. "That I'm seated at the same table with the most captivating woman in the room."

He's smooth. Andrea stilled a nervous twitch over her right eye with a light finger. *Not now of all times.*

He bent slightly at the waist and offered his arm.

Should she tell him an escort was utterly unnecessary? That she was more than capable of locating the table by herself. The words that fell out of her mouth surprised even her. "Thank you," she said, deciding to regard it as a polite gesture for the occasion. Then, tucking her arm under Chet's, she struggled to make sense of the magnetic pull toward a man she barely knew.

When Chet pulled out the chair accompanying the place card, Andrea read her name in a red script font. She smiled a thank you, then held her breath as her eyes drifted to the place next to hers. The card read *Chet Taylor.*

Chapter 6

Andrea watched as Chet slipped his suit jacket over the back of his chair. Then, without a blink, he introduced them to the other dinner guests seated at their table. What was he thinking? Now everyone seated at their table would assume they were an item, a couple. She should never have let him escort her to the table.

She tipped her head in Chet's direction, keeping her voice low. "Chet, I don't need you to make introductions for me. I'm quite capable of handling that all by myself. I wouldn't want people to assume we're anything more than mere acquaintances."

He placed his water glass on the table and smacked his lips dry. "Just trying to be helpful. No crime in that, is there?"

The look on his face told Andrea he'd meant every word. Was he blind to the message he was sending? It was time to share a piece of truth about herself. The last thing Andrea wanted was a man doting on her all night, handsome or not. "You should know that I'm practically married to my work." Andrea prepared herself for another one of his long whistles, but he shot her a skeptical look instead, then loosened the knot in his skinny tie.

"Practically? he asked, "that does sound serious." He scanned the room, then turned and looked at her. "It may surprise you, but I'm not intending on proposing to you tonight."

She felt the heat of embarrassment in her cheeks. Inhaling to the count of four, Andrea drew from her meditation practice to slow her hammering heart. "You know I wasn't implying anything of the sort."

Chet released a measured exhale. "Work can be satisfying, but it doesn't keep you warm at night."

Andrea had trouble believing what she'd heard. "I don't intend to be rude, Chet, but you're not in a position to tell me what is or isn't right for my life. We just met, and frankly, it's none of your business. I'm trying to be honest with you and avoid giving you the wrong impression."

"And what might that impression be?"

Were her eyes deceiving her, or was a look of innocence washing over his face? Andrea sighed. The situation was getting more complicated. "You know what I'm trying to say. I don't want to lead you on. I'm not dating because I'm focusing on my career." That was, in part, the truth. It was easy to get lost in her work after her marriage ended. Even though four years had passed since her divorce, a part of her secretly believed she wasn't enough for Ben, so why would she be enough for anyone else?

He handed her the breadbasket, blessedly interrupting her thoughts, then gave her a quick once over. "Roll? Although, it doesn't appear you eat much."

Unbelievable! Andrea scanned the room, hoping to find an open seat at another table. She couldn't imagine enduring the entire meal next to this Neanderthal. He guessed right about her diet, but she'd rather be the last person standing in this room than let him know it. "I'd love one," she said, pushing her zero-carb diet to the sidelines. She chose a butter croissant and passed the basket to the next guest at their table. He was on if he wanted to play this cat-and-mouse game with her. She opened her eyes wide, then peered at Chet through heavy lashes. "Would you pass the butter, please?"

His fingers fumbled to the butter dish, grazing his water glass and almost tipping it over. "Do you know what would happen to you if I brought you home to meet my parents?"

The reprieve was over as she struggled to run alongside his quick wit. She held her butter knife in mid-air. "Home? Why would you ask such a thing? We've only just met."

Chet handed her the butter, ignoring her question. "My mother would take one look at you, and the first thing she'd set out to do is fatten you up." He followed his statement with a heavy chuckle as if his remark was humorous.

Andrea placed her knife on the small plate and fiddled with her napkin. The man was flabbergasting! She shifted in her seat, unable to find a comfortable spot. And for a good reason! It was impossible sitting next to *Mr. Know It All*. He was the most presumptuous, rude, outspoken man she'd ever met. And she'd met plenty!

"Tell me, why the all-work-and-no-play attitude," he asked, pulling her back to the conversation. He opened his mouth wide, popped an entire roll inside it, and clamped his jaws shut.

She couldn't help but stare at his ability to devour an entire roll with such ease. A dribble of butter rested on the corner of his mouth. She held back the impulse to wipe it away.

He peered back at her.

Heat fired up her neck. She touched the corner of her mouth, the same spot as his buttered lips. "You have butter…and to answer your question, I get a lot of satisfaction working with authors and publishers. And my mentor is invaluable to me. I'd be a fool to invest in anything other than my career right now."

Chet licked away the butter. "A fool, huh?"

Andrea rolled her eyes in his direction. She didn't expect a man like Chet to understand her reasoning. All of her earlier assumptions about him were proving to be true. He was a handsome lady's man with a very healthy sense of confidence.

Chet reached for his water glass. "I think I get the picture."

Calm filled her. Finally, maybe Chet did understand her after all. Her shoulders relaxed.

"Sounds like you have everything figured out. You mentioned a mentor?" Chet wiped the corners of his mouth with a napkin.

Andrea pressed her lips together, half-expecting the direction he'd take with his next question. She should have known better than to share too much information about herself.

"Yes, Jim Phillips. He took over steering my career after my father's retirement."

"Is he interested in you?"

Andrea's mouth gaped open. "Jim? That's absurd. He's twenty years older than I am."

Chet's face turned serious, causing Andrea to pause in her defense.

"You don't strike me as a naive woman," he said, then leaned back, allowing enough room for the server to place his salad in front of him on the table.

Andrea slathered an unwanted second layer of butter across her croissant. "Don't be ridiculous," she huffed. *What is it about this man – having her flabbergasted one minute and charmed in the next?*

Chet forked his lettuce greens. "Happens all the time, but I'm not one to judge."

She placed the edge of her knife against the dinner plate, hoping to regain her composure before responding, but Chet filled in the gap before she had the chance.

"You and Lila seem to be close in age. I don't think it'll be long before she and Conrad have kids. So, you may want to give this liaison with Jim a little more thought."

Liaison. Andrea wanted to scream. "That's quite a leap from Lila to me." *The audacity of this man discussing the topic of her future children. And with Jim, of all people, whom she thought of as an uncle with two grown children of his own.*

As she drizzled the raspberry vinaigrette over her salad greens, she knew it was time to turn the table of this conversation. "What about you, Mr. Taylor? Are you planning on having a family down the road?"

Chet's grin widened. "You bet. I'm counting on at least three, maybe four, kids. They bring fun back into life, not that I'm not guilty of having too much of that as it is," he said, raising a suggestive eyebrow.

Andrea threw him a tight smile. She could only imagine what he'd meant by that and hoped he wasn't about to fill her in on the details. She assumed their conversation was over, but he'd managed to surprise her with the words that came next.

"It's finding someone with the same priorities for life that I find challenging." He wiped his plate clean with his last lettuce leaf and then asked for a second roll.

His statement struck Andrea as a bit old-fashioned for his type. Unless she was wrong about him. She decided to probe for more. "You sound like an expert on the topic of having kids."

He shook his head. "Nope, not an expert, but I've experienced enough with my brother's kids and love how fun they are. I can only imagine it'll be tenfold with my own. I'm excited for what's coming next in my life."

"I can't imagine building a family without a wife. Anyone special in mind?"

He tilted his head and gave her a wink, implying they'd crossed a line into the next level of their relationship. "Ms. Lockhart, are you asking me if I have a girlfriend?"

Andrea's back stiffened. *What am I doing?* Of course, that's how it must've sounded to him, but she refused to let him ruffle her and decided to wait him out.

"I dated Olivia Hawkins for a while. She's an attorney in Sturgeon Bay. She's here tonight."

Andrea sipped from her water glass. "You talk as if she's part of your past."

He nodded. "Because she is."

"What happened?" With the limelight in his direction, Andrea's shoulders relaxed.

He turned to face her. His ocean-hued eyes captivated hers, stealing her breath. She could imagine how many hearts he'd broken along the way. "Not a good fit."

Andrea leaned toward him, then rested her chin on

laced fingers. She studied the man sitting next to her. He blew hot then cold. She wanted to know more, to understand the man behind the beautiful eyes. "What do you mean?"

"Don't misunderstand. Like most people, I enjoy an occasional night out, but Olivia prefers dining at Door County's finest. I'm content with a thick steak on the fire pit in my backyard with a dozen good friends. Half the time, she and I struggled to make conversation unless, of course, it involved her day at work."

Andrea's heart softened. Chet painted Olivia as a bit self-absorbed, but her drive in her career sounded much like her own. "I don't believe it's wrong to talk about your career as long as it's reciprocal. It's more about balance than anything else."

Chet grunted. "Olivia didn't get the whole farming way of life. She most certainly didn't enjoy hearing about how I had to mend fencing all afternoon or turn over a crop that had gone bad. And forget about my dreams for the place. You showed more interest in my work in our earlier conversation than she ever did."

Andrea could relate. Before Ben, she'd met her fair share of unsuitable partners. "It's interesting, isn't it, to recognize that undeniable sense of loneliness when you're with the wrong person?"

He nodded. "Olivia loves her work and the nightlife. But, after that, there's nothing much left for anyone or anything else but a good time."

"What kept you together?" She asked and then finished the last of her salad.

"She catches your eye if you understand my meaning, then holds it for a while."

Why am I surprised? "Of course." She should have

known he'd place high marks on an attractive woman.

Chet shrugged. "You've got to have some chemistry, but you need a lot more to make it work for a lifetime."

He'd raised a good point. Chemistry was essential, but a strong interest in each other's wellbeing was also crucial. Andrea had that once and hoped it would come again for her one day. Lately, she was beginning to wonder. Andrea's gaze moved to Lila and Conrad. "I wouldn't argue with that. Lila and Conrad appear to be a good example of what you're talking about."

"No doubt. I wish what Conrad found with Lila is out there for all of us."

Andrea sighed, wanting to agree with him once again. Would she ever find that kind of love again? Her thoughts drifted as the waiters served the entrees. Despite her earlier impression, Chet's willingness to stand behind his beliefs moved him from annoying to admirable. He would wait for the right partner to share life with, even if it meant being alone for as long as it took. Chet Taylor was his own man despite his numerous flaws and less-than-subtle remarks.

Andrea made pleasant conversations with those around her during dinner. When coffee and dessert arrived, Chet leaned toward her as she scooped the peak off the whipped cream sitting atop a piece of Door County cherry cheesecake.

His voice hit her ears as velvety as the cream in her mouth. "Is it real or imitation?"

"Oh, it's real, all right, but I'd expect nothing less tonight. The entire day so far has been nothing short of magical."

"You're right about that. I'd place the dinner at a

ten. That roasted duck hit the spot. What is your opinion on the salad?"

"The salad? Delicious. Did you notice my plate?"

"You mean the one you licked clean?" Chet asked under his breath.

So now he's being cautious about what others think? Andrea scowled. "I did no such thing."

He chuckled, giving her the impression she'd entertained him somehow. "The greens came from Taylor Farms."

Now that was impressive. Andrea brought her hands together. "How do you manage to provide fresh produce over winter?"

He finished the last of his coffee, wiped his mouth with his napkin, and placed the cup on the saucer. The man had a healthy appetite.

"With Conrad's help last year, we replaced a couple of our greenhouses. With a little good luck, that opened the door to what I hope is the future."

Luck? Andrea doubted that contributed much. She could almost reach out and touch his passion for the farm. "You mean moving to an all-organic line?"

"Yup. We'd double our profits. I have a few other ideas for the farm as well."

Andrea knew without asking that Chet wouldn't push his father down a road he wasn't ready to go down. But she didn't understand his hesitation. Had something happened? "What's stopping you?"

"Dad's opposed to any growth," Chet continued, "including our newest venture. After we repaired the main house after storm damage, we turned it into a bed and breakfast causing some debt. I'm hoping for a strong revenue stream from that baby."

It was hard not to be impressed. Besides all Chet accomplished, his steadfast patience with his father truly touched her, but to the point of stagnating his own dreams for the business. That didn't make sense to her. A piece to the puzzle was missing. "You said earlier that your farm services most of the county. I assume you have extra produce? Where does that go?"

"That's a story for another occasion. One I hope I get to explain to you."

Andrea threw him a doubtful look. "I don't see how that'll be possible. After tonight, we'll never see each other again."

"I'm going to go with my gut instinct here and tell you there's a reason why we met tonight."

Andrea huffed. "Oh, for goodness sake."

Chet's hand was at the back of her chair, assisting her before her feet were in motion.

She smiled at the other guests as she rose from the table. "I could use some fresh air. If you'll all excuse me," she said.

~

Chet watched Andrea walk away from him, wishing she'd asked him to join her. His spirits fell as fast as the paper confetti sprinkling on the newly-married couple who were making their way to the dance floor. He thought dinner had gone smoothly. *Was I wrong?*

It had been a long time since a woman caught his attention the way Andrea Lockhart had managed to do. He found her intelligent, feisty enough to put his toes to the fire, and interested in his passion for the farm. She was one of the most engaging women he'd met in a long time. And yes, she was also attractive. He couldn't deny that. He wanted to get to know her better if she'd let him.

The fact that she was married to her work concerned him. Is she another Olivia? It didn't sound like it if she had family and children included in her future.

Chet resumed his seat at the table and focused on the facts. She was still here. While he continued to try putting the pieces together of this captivating woman, he lifted the coffee carafe and refilled his cup, offering the same to those seated around him.

"She's a beautiful girl," Mrs. Perkins said. Chet placed the familiar voice to his middle school teacher seated across from him.

Chet looked up and smiled into the instructor's eyes, who had challenged his seventh-grade math skills.

"That she is, but she told me tonight, she's almost married to her work."

She gave him the same skeptical look when reviewing his algebraic answers. "Almost doesn't sound as certain as it implies."

Chet hit the brakes on his train of thought. Maybe his instincts were right, and they had met for a reason. He'd have to rely upon his gift of spontaneity. With dinner over, the evening would segue into the dance. Although he wasn't privy to her plans, he expected her to return to the table. He didn't consider himself a quitter and had proved that fact by recommitting himself to the farm. He saw no reason to back down now.

Chapter 7

Andrea rubbed the goosebumps on her arms, regretting the decision to step outside without a coat. The crisp December air worked its magic, clearing her thoughts. The conversation with Chet over dinner was both irritating and intriguing. Chet's relationship with Olivia Hawkins hadn't worked out for traditional reasons. Andrea was intrigued. Was it her career or a general disinterest in having a family that ruined things between them? Andrea had known many women who devoted their lives to their careers and appeared happy for it.

When she stepped back inside, the soft tones of violins playing caught her attention. A three-piece band, dressed in white winter suits and Christmas red cummerbunds, were warming up on the far side of the room. She smiled at the adorable sight. Lila and Conrad hadn't missed a detail.

The tables had been pushed aside in her absence, transforming the space from the dining room to more of a lounge feel. Lila and Conrad had center stage in the opening dance of the evening. Andrea's feet slowed. If she questioned their love at any moment, and shamefully she had, that suspicion was gone. The look between them told her their search for true love was over. Andrea scanned the room. Her eyes stopped at Chet. When his hand moved to the back of her chair, she understood the silent request. Her heart softened in this small yet considerate gesture. Before making a decision, she walked toward him, finding it impossible not to return his smile. A flood of comfort filled her with each step bringing him closer to her.

"I took the liberty of ordering you a cold beverage."

"Thank you, Chet. That was very thoughtful."

"Don't forget you promised me the first dance, but before I can take you out on the floor, I'd like to dance with the bride. It's tradition."

Tradition? What did he mean? Her eyes followed him as he walked with a purposeful step toward the bride. His face filled with the enthusiasm of someone much younger as he and Lila danced across the room. Andrea struggled with a twinge of jealousy at the life Lila had made for herself here in Sister Bay. One filled with love, friendship, and contentment. Something she certainly didn't have back home. When the music ended, Lila and Chet walked in her direction. She would be next in Chet's arms on the dancefloor, and her heart was already beginning to flutter with anticipation.

"Look who I found," Chet presented Lila with a turn of the hand. She promenaded toward the table as if they were still on the dance floor. Her gown swished around her, the silky fabric settling perfectly against her body.

"Chet, you'll have to take Andrea on the dance floor, and don't take no for an answer. She's quite good." Lila beamed a radiant smile.

Chet's grin widened. "She's already promised me her first dance," he said, not allowing room for argument.

Andrea shot a sideways glance in Lila's direction. "You realize it's been since my sister Hannah's wedding that I last danced the waltz. It's not like I can get out there and wiggle my way through it."

"I wouldn't mind watching you try," Chet added.

Andrea rolled her eyes in Chet's direction.

Lila waved her concern away with a flick of her hand, then turned toward Andrea. "Before you go anywhere, I'm dying to talk with you."

Lila pulled out a chair while Chet walked in the direction of his friends. It was hard not to notice his confident stride as he walked across the room.

"He's something else, isn't he?" Lila's eyebrows rose.

To Andrea, it sounded more like a statement than a question. "He certainly is."

"He's one of the good ones, Andrea."

Andrea forced a light laugh. "I'm not husband shopping at your wedding, and please, no matchmaking."

Lila sighed. "For reasons unknown to me, we both know you're not dating. That alone tells me you need all the help you can get."

Even though she was right, Andrea scrambled for a response. "That's not true. What about Nick?"

Lila chuckled. "Are you kidding me? That was last year's Christmas party. From what I remember, you never went on a second date."

Andrea's shoulders slumped. *She's right.*

"I hope you're not using what happened in your past to stop you from moving forward. I don't want you to settle for anything less than wonderful."

Lila's soft tone comforted Andrea, but the last thing

she wanted to talk about tonight was the divorce that changed everything for her. *Is that where Lila's headed?* Over the years, it had been a familiar topic for the two friends. The light pressure of Lila's hand drew her eyes to settle on her dear friend's face.

"Your divorce was not your fault."

Andrea groaned. "I know. Ben was an admirable man. His passion for helping others overrode everything, even our marriage." She didn't tell Lila that she wasn't sure if she could take the chance on love again. It hurt too much. Her ears perked with Chet's laughter. She spotted him across the room and indulged in the distraction.

"Andrea, if we're willing to follow God's lead, we all get another chance in life to make things right. Look at Conrad and me."

Lila's urging pulled Andrea back to the conversation. A sigh escaped her. Andrea had tried prayer, and even that didn't work. Lila and Conrad's love had rekindled, but Andrea accepted that second chances in love don't come along for everyone. So, she told herself she was content working the extra hours and on weekends. A lot of good that did for her. She's right back to job searching.

The concern on Lila's face didn't waver. "When do you have to go back to New York?" she asked.

Andrea threw her a puzzled look, unsure where their conversation would go next. "Monday morning."

What happened next reminded Andrea of their brainstorming sessions. Lila's face would light up with an idea. Her fingers would glide across the keyboard as if it might escape her. She had the same look now, only this time it had everything to do with Andrea and not one of her scenes.

Lila lowered her voice. "Would you consider changing your plans and staying a little longer? This transition from women's fiction to children's lit isn't as easy as I thought. I could use your help."

Andrea couldn't remember Lila having a problem in the writing department, but maybe the jump in genres was more difficult than she expected. "You're having a few problems?"

Lila nodded. Concern washed over her face threatening to rain on the bride's perfect day.

Andrea's professional instincts kicked in, wanting to help her friend, and there was no reason to rush back.

Lila scooted toward her, perched at the edge of her chair. "Listen, all I'm suggesting is that you stay a few more days until I return from my honeymoon."

Andrea felt her brow furrow. "But that's later next week, isn't it?"

Lila nodded as if a few days and a week meant the same amount of time. "Remind me of your last vacation."

Andrea returned a blank look, recalling a similar argument with the office manager before leaving New York.

"That's what I thought," Lila said in a matter-of-fact tone. "You could stay, and you know it. It might be good to get out of the routine and enjoy yourself before tackling a new job search. Door County is a wonderful get-a-way."

Andrea forced a laugh. "Jim and I carved out some time to tackle year-end accounting work. I'm not sure how he'll handle an extended stay. You remember how precise he is about things."

Lila swooshed Andrea's concern away with a flick of her hand. "Jim will understand."

She's right. Andrea leaned into her chair and realized her argument was losing its strength fast. "Even if I wanted to, which I haven't agreed to yet, I couldn't find accommodations. The hotel is booked up with a family reunion. They asked me this morning if I could check out early."

Lila waved a frantic hand in Chet's direction. "Hold that thought."

Andrea reached for Lila's arm. She assumed Chet would wander off with his friends for the remainder of the evening or scoop up one of the attractive women to tote on his arm. But, instead, he shot Lila a wide grin. "Lila, what are you doing?"

Now that Lila had Chet's attention, she motioned him back to their table. "Trust me. I've got a great idea."

As soon as Chet rejoined them, he pulled out a chair and took a seat next to Andrea at the table. "What do you need, Mrs. Hamilton? Another dance?"

Lila silenced his question with a dazzling smile. "Conrad mentioned that you're still looking for an innkeeper for the B&B."

Chet nodded. "Dad called me earlier about this very issue. We found our candidate, but there's one problem – she can't start right away. So, for the short-term, we're still stuck. Why do you ask?"

Lila folded her arms across her chest. Her stunning new diamond sparkled after catching the attention of the lights. "I think I may have found a temporary solution for you."

Andrea swallowed hard, knowing Lila as well as she did and fearing where this was headed – straight in her direction.

"I could use a quick fix on this one. The B&B has reservations next week, and a few more are waiting for confirmation. Our problem is I'm busy running the farm. Dad does what he can, but he's down to half-days since his stroke. Finding someone to fill in until our gal can start has become our top priority."

Lila's eyes landed on Andrea.

Oh no. Andrea's stomach flipped in circles. Her suspicion of what came next was about to come true.

"Andrea's considering extending her stay, but the nearby hotels are all booked. I think she might be able to help you out, at least for the short term."

Andrea pressed a finger to still her eye twitch which was right on cue. "What?" She heard the croak in her voice, drawing the attention of guests from a nearby table. She turned a shoulder to block the scolding looks.

Chet hid a chuckle behind the back of his hand. "Oh, I'm sure Ms. Lockhart would prefer to stay at Birchwood Lodge."

Lila nodded. "That would be her preference, but a family reunion is about to land in our little village."

Chet slapped the table with a firm hand. "That's right. They come up from Milwaukee every year. It's quite the bash. In fact, we're already getting orders to accommodate the restaurants with their orders."

Lila beamed. "Andrea needs lodging, and you need a temporary innkeeper. I did my good deed for the evening as far as I'm concerned. It's a match. Plus, you're two of my favorite people in this room. I'm sure you can work things out."

Andrea pressed the flat of her hands against the table's edge, preparing to plead her case. "I appreciate your quick thinking, Lila, but I don't know the first thing about running a bed and breakfast. I don't even eat breakfast!" She was shrieking now but didn't care if others heard her. Despite her friend's insistence, she had to find a way to stop this ludicrous idea. She didn't know the difference between a teaspoon and a tablespoon despite her mother's best efforts. How would she ever handle making breakfast for a small crowd? Oh, no, no, no. This whole idea had to be stopped.

Lila gave her a side look. "Oh, yes, you do eat breakfast. We loved the scones at Champs, remember? And what about George's in Greenwich? Don't tell me you've forgotten about the eggs benedict specials we enjoyed every first Sunday of every month?"

Chet bent his head in Andrea's direction. "If I were you, I wouldn't start an argument with the bride. Not with Conrad heading this way." He thumbed at Conrad striding toward them with hurried steps.

Andrea released an exasperated sigh. "Oh, for goodness sake, that's not a reason to go along with this. You have no idea what you're getting yourself into here."

"I trust Lila. She must have a good reason to suggest it. At this point, I'll take anyone. I'm in a desperate situation."

Did I hear him correctly? The man flat-out insulted me. Andrea gritted her teeth, despite the amusement in Lila's eyes.

Chet got to his feet and slid the chair back under the table. "As I see it, Andrea, we both have a problem that needs a solution. Maybe Lila's right, and it is temporary. When our girl shows up, you're off the hook."

"Of course, I'm right." Lila wore a triumphant smile

as if she had solved two problems with one solution.

Andrea had to say something to turn this whole idea around. "You don't understand, Chet. I'm the queen of take-out, not frying bacon for a houseful of guests."

Chet released a hearty laugh. He gestured to an imaginary scene behind his shoulder. "Didn't you tell me that you could still taste the blueberry waffles your Aunt Linda made for when you were a kid?"

Andrea shook her head, "But she made them, not me."

Chet's eyes crinkled with a smile. "How hard can it be?" he asked. "And you have me if you need any help."

Andrea's mouth dropped open. So, he was going along with this plan? How could he be so calm about this? But then, she remembered his patience with his father and her heart softened.

"Running the inn is a snap, and you're already a seasoned marketer. I'm sure you'll develop new strategies to improve the operation. Think of it as a challenge. Besides, we'll support you a hundred percent." Then Chet added the deal-breaker, "Don't forget, you earn free room and board."

It took all of Andrea's grit and will to remain quiet. He just explained he and his father were too busy to run the B&B. What kind of support did he imagine he'd provide? This idea of Lila's was a disaster, but as hard as Andrea searched for a way out, she came up empty. Lila needed her help, Chet and his father needed an innkeeper, and the hotel was full. The bottom line was she did have the time. The office was closed for the holiday season.

Lila's voice softened. "It'd be nice to spend some time with you before going back to New York. Please stay."

Andrea heard the plea in her friend's voice. A quiet voice whispered for her to pause and give this offer some thought before rushing to a decision. Maybe Lila was right.

"Waffles are what my husband would call a slam dunk," Lila said, with a smile befitting a new wife. "I can share a few of my scone recipes with you tomorrow at the gift opening if you need them."

Andrea sighed. She never imagined a need to collect recipes. She could see the smiles on her mother and Aunt Linda's faces. They'd encouraged her for years to join them in the kitchen. Her shoulders met the back of her chair. "I appreciate the offer, Chet, but I'd like to give this some thought if you don't mind." Maybe later, she would have some time to investigate other options before committing to run his B&B. She could still stay on for Lila, but the B&B sounded too daunting.

Chet raised his palms while Lila looked as satisfied as a fat cat hiding a secret. "No harm giving you some time to get used to the idea. You can let me know, but the sooner, the better so my dad can get some sleep at night."

Andrea widened her eyes. Now he was using his father as leverage? How could she possibly refuse an older man his rest?

Conrad finally approached, blessedly interrupting the conversation. He placed his hands on Lila's shoulders and gazed at her and Chet. "Sorry, you two, but I'm going to have to steal my bride. I have an insistent grandmother waiting to share the family secrets with the newest member of our clan."

"We understand," Andrea said, hoping Chet didn't

notice she was speaking for both of them. A sin she'd nearly bit his head off earlier during dinner.

Conrad gestured to the dance floor. "What are you two doing sitting at the table? Get out there! This is one of our favorite songs." Lila agreed with a smile and nod, encouraging the pair to take the floor.

Andrea recognized the movement of a waltz and noticed that the dance floor was already half-full. She expected that would be enough to discourage Chet.

"You got it, buddy," Chet said, assuming Andrea would join him. He offered Andrea his hand, wearing a triumphant smile that told the world he'd landed a lifetime opportunity. "Looks like Conrad gave us our cue."

"You certainly don't give up, Mr. Taylor," Andrea said.

Chet's eyebrows rose. "Me? No, not often."

More like never, you mean. Andrea placed her hand in his and rose from her chair.

Chapter 8

Chet made minor adjustments to his steps as they glided across the room. With the tables now pushed to the side, there was plenty of room for dancers to sashay their partners, some going as far as to include dips. He maneuvered them with ease, applying the slightest pressure on Andrea's back to navigate them around the other dancers. He had a natural style allowing her to relax in his arms and follow his lead.

Andrea smiled up at him. "You certainly know how to impress a lady on the dance floor."

"I do what I can," he said, clearly appreciating her compliment.

"Where did you learn to dance? You don't look the type."

He threw his head back and laughed, a sound she was beginning to enjoy. For a split second, she feared his response was too bold. Then she remembered who she was dancing with – Chet.

"I didn't know there was a type, but I'm glad you're curious about me." He flashed her a devilish grin. "In all honesty, I was the one my aunts would drag out onto the dance floor at a family wedding. So, I couldn't help but learn under their tutelage. And you?"

"It's been years since I've danced. The last time was at my sister's wedding, but the groomsman I was paired up with had two left feet."

Chet chuckled, "Makes for a long night."

"If I remember correctly, he compared dancing to cleaning a fresh catch of fish." She giggled, expecting to get another laugh from Chet.

Instead, his steps slowed, causing their timing to fall short of the next beat.

Andrea wondered if he had misstepped.

"What's the problem with cleaning fish? Conrad and I managed to scale it down to under an hour this past summer."

Andrea had no idea he and Conrad were fishing buddies.

They danced in silence for the next few moments, providing a reprieve for Andrea, then Chet broke the silence. "I'm glad you're not fighting me."

She threw him a puzzled look. "What do you mean by that?"

"Many women insist on leading, which is the man's job on the dance floor."

They picked up speed, and Andrea's feet barely tapped on the floor before preparing for the next beat. Her heart was racing, but she followed his lead step-for-step. She hadn't danced like this in years! Then a question swirled around in her head. When they resumed a slower pace, she decided to satisfy her curiosity about the man holding her in his arms. "Does your opinion on a dance floor segue into your personal life?"

He peered into her eyes, "I don't follow. What are you asking?"

She gazed back at him, testing the waters before

asking the question. "Was it Olivia's dedication to her work that caused problems between you or your expectations of her?"

His nostrils flared as the second stanza of music began. "We had different ideas on more than one issue."

Andrea couldn't help herself. "Her career wasn't a problem then?" she asked.

He avoided her gaze.

Did I hit a nerve?

"It was hard to see starting a family with someone who refused to talk about the subject." He raised his arm and led her into a nine-count turn in front of him. When she faced him again, he reached for her free hand and guided them back into the flow of the other dancers.

"So, you *did* have a conversation about children." A victorious smile spread across her face. *Have I managed to rile him?*

She felt his body tense as he peered down his Romanesque nose at her. She should have known better than to antagonize *this* man.

"Only topically, which is more than I can say for you. From the sounds of it, you've put off starting a family or dating, for that matter. Or, maybe I misunderstood you, and you prefer not to have a family and children one day."

Andrea huffed. "What makes you think I don't want children? They've always been a part of my plan for life."

"It's hard to start a family when you're married to your work. Your words, may I remind you."

She stomped her foot like a child in her mind. "Touché," she mumbled, but his remark rang true. She had pushed away dreams of having children when her marriage ended. "There are times when dreams have to wait." *Does Chet have a point?*

"As long as you don't wait too long," Chet said. The last measure of music was fast approaching. Chet maneuvered her in a reverse turn with an uncertain look, bringing a smile to her face and changing the tone between them. It wasn't long before they both broke out in laughter, having pulled off the pattern. After that, it became easier. One dance led to another, then a few more after that. A thin layer of sweat dotted her forehead by the end of the first set as they made their way back to the table. Excitement buzzed in the room as everyone took their seats in preparation for the grand march and the introduction of the bridal party.

Chet tipped his head in her direction. "Would you like something to drink?"

Andrea dabbed at her brow with a tissue from her purse. "What a fabulous idea. Whatever you're having is fine with me."

He rose from the table and spoke over his shoulder, grinning as he walked into the crowd, "I'll bring doubles."

It was impossible not to enjoy his playfulness. "Chet," Andrea scolded, "Don't you dare! You'll look like the wait staff."

Ten minutes later, Chet stretched his long legs out in front of him, wearing a look as if seated in front of a warm fire. Andrea's shoulders fell, feeling relaxed in Chet's company. She sipped from a tall glass of iced tea and moved her attention to the announcer. She watched the matron of honor and best man walk around the dance floor. Their faces flushed with unwanted attention. As the couple pulled to the side, the lights dimmed, causing a hush to spread across the room.

The music started as a whisper, silencing the chatter among the guests. The lights lifted, reminding Andrea of a fresh sunrise at her Aunt Linda's farm. Conrad stood on the dance floor. His broad shoulders were firm. His hands were comfortably at his sides. His face reflected an inner peace with the promises he'd made today to Lila and before God.

Anticipation in the room caused Andrea's arms to chill. She rubbed the goosebumps away until Chet placed his suit jacket over her shoulders. Was it his smile or the coat that caused the warmth that spread throughout her body? Movement in the room stilled as everyone's attention locked in on Conrad, waiting for his bride.

A second light ebbed into focus as if they were all in a dream. It illuminated Lila, standing directly across from her groom. Her smile slowly drew the same conclusion – true love had materialized right before everyone's eyes. They walked toward one another as if casting aside their old life and stepping toward the new. Conrad offered his hand, symbolizing their union. Lila slipped into his arms, and with the change in music, their feet moved together as they began to dance.

Conrad led Lila on the dance floor, not with Chet's skilled expertise but with the determination of a man in love trying to please his new bride. It was evident to everyone that he struggled to keep time with the music, but the tears in Lila's eyes washed away his mistakes. Andrea wiped the moisture away from the corners of her own eyes. She looked around the room, realizing she wasn't the only one affected by the scene. When she glanced at Chet, he lifted the corners of his mouth, sharing the moment with her. As burly as this man was, he had been touched by it all.

Before the dance had a chance to end, the newly wedded couple faced thunderous applause. Moments later, the guests were invited back to the dance floor to enjoy the second music set. Andrea rose from her chair, intending to call it a night. But when Chet rolled up his sleeves and offered her his hand, hesitation stopped her.

He threw her one of his contagious smiles as if he'd read her thoughts. "Let's enjoy ourselves, shall we?" he asked. "This time, you've got a man who can dance."

The temptation to say yes was overwhelming. Over the last hour, Andrea's earlier impressions of Chet had changed. There was an inner peace about him she admired. It drew her toward him. Had he found something in life that she was still searching for? Chet raised his brows, reminding her he was waiting for an answer. Andrea inhaled a big breath. It was a magical evening, and a big part of her didn't want it to end.

Andrea rose to accept his hand. They danced to a medley of songs, one barely finishing before the other began. Electricity filled the air like the finale in a Fourth of July fireworks display. Andrea couldn't remember the last time she'd lost track of time as she had tonight. It almost felt as if Chet managed to set free the woman she used to be, the one before her career took over her life. People who knew her back home would have thought her to be outrageous as she swung to the beat of the music, matching Chet's footwork step-for-step. Before long, the night began to wind down, filling Andrea with an unwelcomed pang of regret. Her Cinderella evening was about to come to an end.

Chapter 9

A few minutes before midnight, the wait staff began offering refreshments in long-stemmed glasses to the guests. Probably to help usher in the New Year, Chet thought. Lila and Conrad took center stage and toasted their guests, wishing them prosperity and happiness in the year ahead. The announcement for the bouquet toss followed.

Andrea turned from the dance floor and walked in the direction of their table. "That's my cue to leave."

Chet followed close behind. "Where are you going? It's bad luck not to participate." He had to think of something to keep her from leaving. Like it or not, she was the only hope to get someone at the inn to handle the reservations and the breakfast, even if she couldn't cook.

Andrea released a laugh more forced than those he'd heard earlier.

Chet decided to go out on a limb and ask the question. "Any thoughts on the innkeeper position?"

Andrea looked down at her feet and wiggled her toes after abandoning her shoes earlier in the evening. "I appreciate the opportunity, Chet, but I don't think it's a good idea, even for the short term."

He needed an innkeeper in the worst way. The farm

needed to open on schedule. Chet needed the income to make a dent in the loan payments. "Maybe if you see the place for yourself?" he suggested.

Her shoulders lifted, breathing life into a little bit of false hope.

That's all the wiggle room Chet needed. "OK, let's do it." His eyes darted to the foyer, swelling with single women positioning themselves for the bouquet toss.

Andrea slipped her feet back into her shoes. "You don't mean right now, do you?"

Chet avoided her gaze and reached for his suit jacket from the chair. "That's exactly what I mean."

The drummer started a beat electrifying the group waiting for the bouquet, yet Andrea appeared oblivious to the excitement. Chet scanned the back exit. "Why don't you wait here while I'll get our coats? Then, we can head out the back."

With both coat check tickets in his hand, Chet steered through the crowd working through the bottleneck of expectant brides, picked up the coats, and turned back to retrace his steps. A flurry of frantic screams interrupted his stride. His feet stopped dead in their tracks. Andrea was in full view holding the bouquet. She must have followed him to the coat check and got caught up in the toss.

Her cheeks, the color of the setting sun, reminded him of the rare opportunities on the farm when he witnessed a killer sunset. She looked at him and mouthed, "I don't believe this." Her hair was messed up beautiful after two sets of dancing. Chet gave his head a nod. *Get your head on straight!*

Andrea pressed the small bunch of flowers to her chest. In the next blink of an eye, the little flower girl hurried toward her and wrapped her arms around Andrea's legs, squealing with excitement.

Andrea smiled at the little angel, working her fingers through the little girl's soft curls.

Watching her, something big moved in Chet's heart. He took a step toward them.

"I have no idea how this just happened," Andrea gushed. "I wasn't even part of the group."

"Andrea," Lila called from the foyer. The smile on her face was apparent that she was pleased with the recipient of her bouquet.

Chet released a huff. "I told you that's how important tradition is around here. It doesn't pay to run. It has a way of finding you."

Andrea giggled at his remark. "For a man who can dance to any song thrown at him, you certainly have some old-fashioned ideas."

Before Chet had a chance for a retort, a photographer burst onto the scene. "Turn this way and smile," the young man said. In the next moment, a fireworks flash caught the moment.

When the evening was about to close, Chet lowered his head. "You about ready to leave?"

She nodded. "After we say goodbye to Lila and Conrad."

Chet grinned, recognizing his opportunity. "You mean as a couple, or would you rather go as individuals?"

Andrea released a slow smile telling him she had caught on to his humor.

He raised a hand in his defense. "Don't want to overstep."

"You? Overstep? I can't imagine."

~

Andrea knew even considering taking this temporary post as an innkeeper was a bad idea. First, she'd promised Jim a sit-down meeting to help her sift through some of her accounts which were a total mess. And second, she had to start a brand-new job search. The sooner, the better. Yet, here she was, sitting next to an almost total stranger out in the middle of nowhere, driving to take a look at the inn. She should tell him that she changed her mind, and they should head back. She turned to him, ready to explain the situation when Chet turned off Highway 42 onto a narrow driveway and turned off the truck's headlights. A blanket of darkness settled in around them. *Great. What did I get myself into?* Andrea's heart skipped a beat. "What are you doing?"

"Not sure how long it's been since you've followed the moonlight," Chet said as if that were a passage of life for everyone.

Andrea blinked, allowing her eyes to focus. The inky blackness, the moon's glow, and the sound of pressed stones beneath the tires added to the allure. Chet curled around a corner. A wooden plaque swung in the wind from an enormous oak tree. *Welcome to Taylor Farms B&B.*

"We kept it simple," Chet said before she had the opportunity to ask. "I had one of my buddies carve it from a wood slab from one of our fallen trees."

"Nice touch," Andrea nodded but was soon distracted by the large two-story house coming into view. Single-bulb lights illuminated a pair of windows near the front entrance. A large front porch painted in milky white bounced moonbeams askew into the darkness. Andrea visualized wicker furniture running the length of the house in warmer weather and a book begging to be read, waiting on a cushioned chair. It was charming.

As he continued the tour, he flipped on the low beams breaking her lazy summer afternoon state of mind.

"First impressions?" he asked.

Andrea hummed. "I'm having a hard time believing what I'm seeing."

Chet lifted his foot from the gas, the truck slowing in response. Even though it was dark, she could feel the smile drop from his lips. *He hopes I like it.*

Andrea's hand brushed the sleeve of his coat. "It's OK," she said, hearing him exhale. "It bears a striking resemblance to my Aunt Linda's place."

"The aunt you visited as a kid?"

Andrea nodded. "The very same. I'm getting flooded with wonderful memories right now. This is unbelievable."

"I was hoping you'd feel that way after seeing it."

As they passed the house, a small, shingled building stood off to the side of the road. It reminded Andrea of an old outhouse resisting the fact its time had come and gone. It was close enough to the house yet far enough away for privacy. She leaned toward Chet to get a better view hoping she was wrong. *It can't be.* "Is that what I think it is?"

Chet slid his foot over to the brake and appeared equally confused as he stared out the windshield. "I'm not sure. What do you think it is?"

She imagined the grin on his face. It wouldn't surprise her if an outhouse were one of the eccentric experiences for guests, but that meant someone had to clean and maintain it. *Not me!* "An outhouse?"

"It's not so bad. You'll get used to it over time. And I'll…."

Andrea fought against the smooth, persuasive tones in Chet's voice. "Oh, no, I won't. If that's part of the deal, I'm out."

Chet chuckled, setting free Andrea's torment. "It used to be a smokehouse, but we turned it into a mudroom of sorts. It has a fireplace, bench seating, and toy storage. It'll be nice for the snowmobilers, skiers, and sledders to stow their gear instead of dragging it to their rooms. It helps them and us at the same time."

Andrea's shoulders hit the back of the seat. "Why didn't you tell me that from the start instead of egging me on in the wrong direction?"

"And miss out on watching you squirm? No way," he said as he pulled in front of a small clapboard house with pretty yellow shutters.

"And this?" Andrea asked, imagining a honeymoon suite or private quarters for one of the guests.

"It's the innkeeper's cottage."

Andrea's eyes widened. The simple architecture reminded her of a cottage in a fairytale. "Wow. It's lovely."

"It's cozy and simple. Has a natural stone fireplace and my grandfather's oak desk. What's nice is that it's independent of the main house, so you'll have plenty of privacy."

"So, this is where I'd stay?"

Chet nodded. "Yup."

Even though she didn't want to give Chet the impression she was considering the job, she had to be honest about the cottage. Andrea turned to face him. "It's perfect."

"That's what I want to hear," he said as he backed up the driveway and headed down another path. "So, tell me, how did you end up a literary agent? Lifelong dream?"

Andrea shook her head. "No. I always wanted my own business. Years ago, I hooked my dreams on owning a floral shop. I loved the dirt and plants until a book found its way into my hands. Everything changed after that. It's been a straight-on love affair with words ever since. The choice to become an agent was my father's and seemed to make sense."

"New York isn't the easiest place to start a career. How did you manage it?"

Andrea shrugged. "My father's connections. He helped me land my first job in a small agency. I moved to a not-so-good fit after that. I enjoyed the next position at a larger firm and was comfortable, but Jim convinced me to keep moving forward and introduced me to where I am today."

"Makes sense. What happens now in light of the merger?"

Despite her situation, Andrea smiled. "I have no idea. It's a blank slate once again. Jim is making a few inquiries, and once I get home, I'll be able to start a more aggressive job search which is why I shouldn't ...."

The truck came to a complete stop halting the conversation. She was looking at an enormous steel building. Grey. Metal. Large. It gave off a cold industrial feel compared to the cozy cottage she'd just seen until her eyes caught sight of a pair of oversized bay windows. *Windows in a pole barn?* That didn't make sense to her.

"You're looking at my latest big idea," Chet

whispered.

Andrea inched toward the edge of her seat, hoping for a better view. Was she missing something? Nothing special popped out in front of her. "I can't imagine what's coming next."

"Close your eyes," Chet said, using a whisper of a voice. "I want you at a blank slate in your mind. Forget about everything you've seen so far."

The heat of his body told her he was close. Her ears picked up the strong inhales of his breath. "Weddings." The deep rumbling in his voice caused her heart to batter against her chest.

She opened her eyes and looked into his face inches from her own. "Weddings?" She asked, doing her best to keep her mind on the topic and not his lips.

Chet shook his head. "I'd like to turn this old pole barn into a banquet hall to meet growing demand. For some reason, couples want to get married here. With the B&B, we would be able to accommodate their every need, from rooms to a banquet hall including space for the gift opening the next day. I want to remodel the loft area into a honeymoon suite, but hopefully, that's down the road."

Andrea wasn't surprised. She'd been told about the spring apple blossoms and magnificent fall colors that would surely entice engaged couples to come here for their wedding. "From what I've seen of Door County so far, it's a hidden gem, and your idea could very well be a goldmine."

"Looks like you could be our very first customer."

Now he confused her until her eyes followed his gaze to the bridal bouquet sitting between them on the console.

Andrea gave Chet's shoulder a good jab.

Chet chuckled, then asked, "So, what do you think – will the job work out for you?"

Andrea knew better than to give him an answer right on the spot. Despite Lila's persuasion, she should get on that aircraft waiting for her on Monday morning. She had a job search to begin and accounting work to tally. So, why the hesitation? She couldn't let him down now after taking the time to give her a full tour of the place. She felt pulled in two directions. She answered Chet with the best answer she had right now. "Can I sleep on it?" she asked.

Chet steered the truck back down the driveway. "Sure. Are you planning to go to the gift opening tomorrow?"

Andrea exhaled, quite sure what was coming next. "Yes. I am." There was no doubt in her mind Chet Taylor would be there too. Maybe she could muster the courage to tell him she couldn't accept the job.

Chapter 10

When morning arrived, Andrea stretched long and smiled into the sunlight streaming into the room. She'd left the blinds open last night for this very purpose. Sleeping in was a luxury. She glanced at the clock. *8:15.* Rolling onto her side, she pulled the thick quilt up around her neck, snuggling underneath its warmth, relishing her final moments in the comfortable bed. After the visit to the B&B last night, Chet dropped her off at her car and then followed her back to her hotel. He parked his truck and proceeded to walk her to the front entrance, despite her insistence that it was unnecessary. He'd told her that's not how he escorted a lady home. Moment by moment, hour by hour, she was beginning to understand the person behind the man.

Fighting the urge to doze, Andrea decided to run the idea of extending her trip past Jim. After all, Lila was her biggest client, and merger or no merger, if Lila needed help, Andrea wanted to be there for her. She tossed the quilt aside and slipped on the fuzzy slippers and robe. Then, walking over to the coffee machine on sore feet, she popped in a French Roast pod and pressed *Brew.*

It had been too long since she danced the night away as she did with Chet last night, and her tender feet were proof of it. Andrea gazed out the window as the coffee brewed, now thankful for the privacy the fourth floor allowed her. If she let her mind drift and her imagination take over, she would've believed she'd landed inside a beautiful snow globe. Snowflakes as gentle as a soft spring rain fell from heavy clouds and swirled to their final destination. The large flakes blanketed the roads and treetops in a fresh, pristine powder. Smoke billowed from nearby chimneys, and the repetitive sound of a shovel lifting snow from the pavement almost lulled Andrea back to bed. She was beginning to understand why Lila loved Sister Bay as much as she did. There was an energy present here, so very different from New York's pulse.

Andrea breathed in the coffee's robust scent. There was nothing better than the aroma of coffee first thing in the morning. She turned from the Christmas scene, unplugged her phone from the charger, and pulled out the desk chair. She hit Jim's number and took her first sip. *Mmm, that hits the spot.* As she listened to the rings, her mind wandered to the first time she'd met Chet when he asked her for the honor of the first dance. She caught herself smiling in the mirror. Lila was right. *Chet Taylor is one of a kind, that's for sure.*

"Good morning, Andrea," Jim said.

Jolted from her daydreaming, Andrea placed her mug down on the desk with more force than needed. *Oh no.* Splashes of hot coffee spilled onto the Birchwood Lodge's welcome brochure. Brown dribbles slid down the side of the cup, forming a ring.

Jim must have sensed her agitation. "Is everything all right?"

"Yes, of course, a little clumsy this morning, that's all." She lifted a few tissues from a log cabin dispenser and mopped up the sloppy mess listening to Jim's chuckle.

"That doesn't surprise me. You need at least two cups of coffee in the office every morning. How was the wedding? I wish I could have gone, but I didn't have a choice with the kids in town. They come first. The client second."

Andrea stopped her frenzied cleaning. "Me too," she agreed but was surprised at the hesitation in her voice. Although Lila would've liked it, Jim's parental antenna would've been tuned in, and she never would've met Chet, enjoyed herself as much as she did on the dance floor, or had the chance to see the B&B. "Lila and Conrad outdid themselves. I'm not sure if it was the exquisite dinner, the music, or the atmosphere, but it was magical, pure, and simple."

"Glad to hear it. When does your flight get in? I've penciled a meeting for us on Tuesday morning. Does that work for you? After that, we can buckle down with a new job search and hit the accounting work."

Is that all he wants to hear about the wedding? He certainly is a stickler about not wasting time. Andrea sighed, stalling for a few moments. Lila's suggestion of adding a few days to her trip had wiggled itself into reality, and she'd made a good point. Besides, it was only a few more days than planned, a week at most. "Lila asked if I would extend my stay. She's experiencing some bumps in the road transitioning over to children's lit."

"You'd rather do that than get some irons in the fire here for a new job? And what about the bookkeeping?"

Andrea wavered. He was right. She did agree to work with him on their time off. "We'll still have plenty of time when I get back, won't we?"

The squeak of his chair had Andrea visualizing his back pressing into the button-holed leather upholstery of his chair. His feet perched on the corner of his desk.

"I can see your point, and it's been a while since you've taken a vacation. Just don't stay too long."

Andrea breathed a sigh of relief even though she heard the warning in her mentor's voice. Although she didn't need Jim's approval, she wanted it.

"Will you stay on at Birchwood Lodge?" Jim asked.

"No. There's a big family reunion taking place over the next week. The hotel is booked solid. Lila suggested I step in as a temporary innkeeper at their friend's bed-and-breakfast. Their new hire can't start right away, and I'd get free room and board. It probably doesn't sound like the best fit, but –"

Jim interrupted her with a hearty chuckle. "*You* run a B&B?"

Andrea sipped the last drops from her coffee. "I agree it must sound comical, me of all people. But it's a solution for both of us."

Jim blew an exhaustive sigh into the phone as if *he* were considering the job. "A word of caution here committing yourself to a job you're not qualified to do. It sounds challenging to me and not the best fit for you."

Andrea should've known he'd give her a good dose of parental advice. "You're probably right, but it may be my only alternative."

"Why not cast the net to the surrounding area for other accommodations? See what you find."

Andrea huffed. "You're right. Maybe I should check out the other villages."

"In the meantime, I'll email you our shared accounts

so you can get busy. Let's connect later in the week."

"Thanks for understanding, Jim."

Jim released a light laugh. "You bet. And good luck. You may need it if you end up playing innkeeper."

Andrea giggled. "We'll talk soon."

After the call, Andrea peered out the window, watching the snow swirl into curly cattails. She thought about brewing another cup of coffee but decided to head for the shower. Chet was expecting her answer today, and Jim wanted her to scout around for alternate lodging than the B&B. She'd better get moving.

~

A couple of hours later, Andrea walked into Lila's Aunt Cathy's Tudor-style home to find a packed house. She scanned the room looking for an open seat, but those who arrived early had secured all the chairs. Others settled on the floor or the edge of the stairs. Andrea suppressed a slight twinge of apprehension. *Why didn't I leave earlier?* She didn't spot Chet or any of the other men.

Aunt Cathy walked with a purposeful step toward her, wearing a wide smile. "Hi Andrea, I remember meeting you yesterday somewhere between the cocktail hour and dinner. Lila asked me to keep an eye out for you. Glad you could make it." She held a plate of ham rollups in one hand and an embroidered dishtowel over her shoulder. Her red curls were piled high on her head, and she looked as happy as a mother-of-the-bride could be. Andrea recalled the conversations she had with Lila on how her aunt stepped into the role of mother after her parents' car accident.

Cathy closed the door behind her. "Let me take you to the kitchen to get some food. You look hungry."

"Thank you. I'm famished." Andrea had skipped breakfast on Lila's orders to have an appetite for lunch, and the aroma coming from the kitchen reminded her of home.

Andrea slipped off her coat and waved hello to Lila, seated in the front of the living room surrounded by gifts, flushed with a new bride glow. Andrea followed Cathy into the kitchen.

Cathy wriggled the platter of ham rollups between the potato chips and shrimp dip. "Why don't you hand me your coat and help yourself to a plate? There's a nice variety here. If there's anything else you'd like, let me know, and I'll do my best to find it."

The spicy scent of barbeque hung heavy in the room. Cathy had every surface in the kitchen filled like a summertime picnic. A large cutting board was placed over the sink and held a roaster piled high with hot ham and roast beef. Triple-stacked trays had petite cookies, dense chocolate bars, and torte slices. On TV trays, platters of smoked chubs, cheese, and sausage lined the opposite wall.

It was an aroma worthy of any New York deli. "This is amazing. When did you have time to make all of this?"

Cathy waved away her question as if hosting a houseful of guests was an everyday occurrence. "Oh, I had lots of help. When you live in a tight community like this one, everyone lends a hand and brings a dish. Your arrival is perfect. Lila's about to open gifts. The men are downstairs watching the game."

Andrea pinched her brows together. "The game?"

Cathy shot her questioning glance. "The Green Bay Packers, honey. We're going into the playoffs. It's an important one today."

Cathy's enthusiasm was hard to miss, but Andrea couldn't muster excitement for a game she didn't understand.

Cathy must've picked up on her disinterest. "Not a football fan?" she asked.

"Not really. My dad used to watch the Jets game, but that was long ago."

"You will be soon if you spend any time in Wisconsin. But don't worry about that now. Go ahead and help yourself while the food's hot. I'll put your coat in the back bedroom."

Andrea took Cathy's advice and reached for a plate, hoping Chet was downstairs and she'd have a chance to talk with him. She breathed a sigh of relief when he stepped into the kitchen. Since her conversation with Jim, she had returned to her original decision and decided to go home tomorrow. Dressed in khakis with an ocean blue knit sweater over a polo shirt, Chet gave her a warm smile.

"My mother would be glad to see you're loading your plate. I told her all about you this morning on the drive over here and how you need some fattening up." His voice, now familiar, was welcoming to her ears but not what he claimed to have told his mother. Surely, he was kidding.

Andrea's mouth went from a smile to a frown. "Oh, Chet, you didn't."

Chet's laugh took her back to the dance floor last night and the antics he pulled. He made what could've been a quiet evening into an unforgettable one. She couldn't remember laughing that hard and that often.

Andrea balanced her plate on the edge of the table. "Chet, I'm glad to see you. I wanted to talk to you about the job."

He placed two servings of hamburger noodle casserole dead center on his plate. "My dad was thrilled when I mentioned you might be coming on board. He couldn't be happier. Frankly, neither am I." Before placing a couple of barbequed chicken drumsticks on his plate, he shot her a quick wink, then nodded in the direction of a large blue bowl. "You want to give me a scoop of that potato salad?"

"Bring your plate closer to the bowl," she instructed. She served him a hefty portion, hoping to satisfy his appetite and gain his full attention.

"You ready to be part of our team? You can start tomorrow. We have a couple of days before the first guests arrive." He balanced his full plate in one hand while grabbing utensils.

Andrea found herself right back in the middle of this debate – to stay or leave. She was stuck. A big part of her wanted to stay despite her lack of qualifications to run a B&B to be there for Lila and see her through the problems she mentioned. Earlier, she'd tried to find other accommodations but had come up empty. The truth was, she didn't have to rush back. Andrea sighed, still wrestling with the decision. She gave Chet a half-smile. "You've got a deal."

His face brightened with her answer, but the look that passed between them lit up every alert button in Andrea's head. Was it possible she was beginning to have feelings for Chet? She'd better tread carefully from now on.

"Let me know if you need me to come and pick you up."

Andrea shook her head. "No, I can manage." There

was no turning back now.

The roar of a den of lions traveled up the staircase from the basement.

He nodded toward the stairs. "I've got to get back down there. I'm usually in around five."

Andrea gasped. "Five a.m.? It's still dark at that hour, isn't it?"

"That it is." He nodded, unfazed. "You don't have to be there that early tomorrow, but you'd better get used to it. It takes time to cook a good breakfast for a houseful of guests. Does eight o'clock sound better?"

"Perfect, see you then."

He started down the first couple of stairs but stopped and peeked his head around the doorframe. "One more question. Is your mentor on board with the idea?"

Andrea picked up a pair of utensils and wrapped them in a napkin. "We've touched base on the issue."

"Good. I wouldn't want to be the cause of a rift. See you in the morning."

Andrea lifted her plate from the table, ignoring Chet's fading footsteps.

"Andrea," Lila called.

Andrea was surprised to see Conrad sitting next to her in the front of the room. All the other men were downstairs watching the game. A hill of gifts waited for her attention. "Come and join us. I saved a spot for you right next to Cassie."

Andrea made her way toward the front of the room. Although her life was now more complicated, she'd have to figure out how it would work out later. Right now, she intended on giving her full attention to her best friend and the afternoon that lay ahead for them despite the mountain of problems that waited for her.

Chapter 11

On Monday morning at five minutes after seven, Chet wheeled the creeper out from under the antique sleigh he'd been working on in the shop. The last couple of hours had sped right past him. He pushed against the metal runners as he made his way down one side and up the other. He used a critical eye, examining it for weaknesses.

Satisfied with his progress so far, he wiped the oil from his hands with a shop rag before pouring another cup of coffee. Typically, he had two mugs and called it quits. Today, after a restless night's sleep, he needed a third. His thoughts pestered him all night. It wasn't like him to be bothered by the whims of a woman, but somehow, Andrea Lockhart had managed to get under his skin. Deep.

He heard his stomach growl, reminding him he'd skipped breakfast. He planned to head up to the house before Andrea's arrival to ensure everything looked as it should. Earlier, while plowing the driveway, he realized something special had happened between them the night of the wedding, and he was determined to find out more about her. He downed the last of his coffee, slipped on his insulated jacket, pulled his Green Bay Packer cap over his head, and headed toward the house's lights. Snow backlashed against the door when it opened, blinding him in blizzard-like snow for a moment. He trekked to the house with thirty minutes to spare ahead of her arrival.

He let out a loud groan when he entered the kitchen through the back door. Muddy footprints tracked clear across the room. *Dad.* He was getting more forgetful about things lately. After his stroke, he'd never really been the same. That's why Chet came home. To see the older man through until God called him home. His brother had tracked him down in Vegas, where he'd been floundering from one blackjack table to another, winning just enough to make it through another week. But that was behind him now, and he was trying to make up for every wrong he ever committed, especially to his dad.

Chet slipped off his coat, hung it on the rung behind the door, and then went for the wringer bucket and rag mop. It wasn't until he heard a soft rumble of laughter coming from the other side of the room that he stopped what he was doing.

"It's either a woman or you're working through a problem. Which is it?"

Michael Taylor leaned against the door frame and sipped from a Taylor Farms coffee mug.

"Neither," Chet grunted. He swiped the last of the floor with the mop. "I want the place to look as good as possible when Andrea arrives, not as if we live in a barn. Was that you who tracked mud in here?"

"S'pose so. No one else I could blame it on. Your mother's still in Arizona."

Chet looked at his dad, recognizing the grin he'd inherited and the sense of humor to go with it. His parents had modeled a relationship of innocent bantering, ending in laughter more than argument.

"Couldn't find the rug," his dad said, still pleading his case against the footprints.

Chet nodded. "You're right. I threw that old one out last week. Meant to get a new one, but I've been so damn busy." Chet dumped the bucket of dirty water down the drain and wrung the mop dry.

"If you wouldn't spread yourself so thin, you wouldn't have that problem. Saw you working on that fool sleigh again. For the life of me, I can't understand why you waste your time with oddball projects like that one."

Chet nodded but didn't want to fire up the standing argument with his father – the need to generate new revenue sources for the farm and his dad's preference to keep everything the same. He didn't understand how dire their situation was and believed it would pass in time as it had in the past. Chet knew better. If he was still a betting man, he stack the chips on the side of the sleigh. Chet had tried to explain his strategy to his dad, but he didn't think as clearly since the stroke.

"All *this* for the new girl?" his dad asked, pulling Chet back to the conversation.

"She's not a girl, Dad. Her name is Andrea Lockhart. She was a literary agent but lost her job because of a merger. We happened to catch her between jobs, and she was willing to help us out."

"A literary what?"

"She was Lila's book agent."

"*Hmpf.* So why all the fuss for a booking agent?"

Chet sighed. As hard as he tried, there were times he felt he couldn't get through to his dad. "Just want to make a good first impression, that's all."

"Uh-huh. You keep telling yourself that, son, but I know you better than that. What time are you expecting her?"

Chet returned the bucket and mop to the broom closet and closed the door. "Eight."

Dad shuffled his slippered feet toward the sink. "It's almost that now."

Chet followed his dad's gaze to the rooster clock above the sink. The doorbell rang. She was right on time.

~

Andrea pulled the lamb's wool collar of her coat tight around her neck as the wind whipped across the yard. Chet said she should be at the inn at eight o'clock, and she had made it on time. She'd left her luggage in the car assuming she'd have time to retrieve it later. Shifting her weight from one foot to the other, she pressed the small vanilla-colored button again.

The entry door swooshed opened. Chet greeted her with a smile and pushed the storm door out wide. "Good morning, Andrea. Come on in."

Chet's shirt sleeves were cuffed, exposing firm forearms. A bead of sweat lined his brow as if he had just finished a morning run. What on earth had he been doing?

"Good morning, Chet." Andrea returned his smile and walked through the door into a large foyer. She stepped onto the *Welcome* mat that protected a stunning maple floor. The scent of wood hung heavy in the air. It was then she remembered the renovations on the inn. She'd always admired the aesthetic beauty of timber and attributed that preference to her grandfather, a finish carpenter by trade. Looking down at her boots and then at Chet, she lifted her eyebrows in a question. There was no way she'd walk on his beautiful floor with wet boots.

"You can place them right here on the rug," he said, answering her implied question. He closed the door behind her and reached for her coat. "I'll give you the grand tour, as my dad calls it. Coffee?"

Andrea slipped out of her boots and into the flats she'd brought. "That sounds wonderful, but I was up before six this morning and had two cups already. I didn't sleep the best, but I never do when starting a new project." She tucked her gloves in her coat pockets before handing the wrap over to Chet.

A look of surprise crossed his face. "You don't seem the anxious type."

"I wouldn't call it anxiety. Excitement, maybe. Lots of adrenaline," she said through a smile.

A soft chuckle escaped the shadows from across the room. Andrea steered her attention toward the voice and matched it with an older version of Chet. The resemblance between the two men was undeniable.

"We can use a little excitement around here." The older man shot Chet a quick look, then returned his gaze to Andrea. "Michael Taylor. Chet's dad." He placed a mug of hot coffee in her hand.

Andrea cupped her hands around the mug, not wanting to refuse the elder Taylor's kind gesture. The warmth coming from the cup warmed her hands instantly. "Thank you, Mr. Taylor."

"Call me Mike. Seems we'll be getting to know each other a bit while you're here."

Andrea returned the smile and could see where Chet had inherited his good looks. An older pair of the same sea-colored eyes held her captive. Although softer now, a once strong frame and a kind smile appeared to be strong trademarks of Taylor genes. His thinning silver hair was cut in a smooth style, framing his oval face. The same rough, calloused hands as his son reached for her in a firm handshake.

"I'm looking forward to it. I hope Chet was honest with you about my cooking." She gave Mike a nervous smile.

"I trust Chet knows what he's doing." He slipped a quick wink in his son's direction.

The wink! This is how Chet must have learned how to use it so effectively.

"I'll let you two carry on. I'm heading down to the office. We've got a couple of shipments heading out today," Mike said.

"I know. I'll be down later," Chet reassured him.

"I'll need your help processing the orders. You know how much I hate that new machine of yours. Another change you insisted on if I remember correctly."

"It's a computer, Dad." Chet threw Andrea a knowing smile.

"Right," Michael moaned. "Nice to meet you, Andrea."

"Thank you, Mike. Likewise."

It wasn't until Mike turned and left the room that Andrea noticed a slight limp in his gait.

Chet ran a hand along the edge of his face. His *unshaven* face. She took a measured inhale and realized this was how he would look first thing in the morning.

He threw her a questioning look giving her the impression he had the power to read her thoughts. Andrea brought the mug to her lips, now grateful for the coffee in her hand.

"Where would you like the tour to start this morning? With the inn or the cottage, you'll be staying in?"

"The inn." She busied her eyes away from his face and searched for paper and pencil from her bag. *I'd better take notes.*

"You're not going to need to write anything down. It's not that complicated."

Her hands paused. She was so out of her element here. How much did Chet think she knew about running an inn? "You sound confident I can do this job."

"I'm pretty good at reading people. Come on," he nudged.

She followed him down a narrow hall leading them into a newly remodeled room. A natural stone fireplace rose from the floor to the ceiling. A large projection screen consumed most of the available space on the opposite wall, while country farmhouse sofa tables provided plenty of room for drinks and phones and two sets of oak TV trays. The light in the room came from a ceiling fan and sofa lamps, and an enormous bank of windows.

Chet's cell phone buzzed. "Excuse me a second," he said and turned to take the call. "This is Chet. Yes, I'm aware of last month's late fee. Yes, I'm aware I missed last month and the reason for the fee. Hmm, hmm. This month looks good. I appreciate the call."

Andrea wished she could have been anywhere but where she was. She had to ask. "Is everything OK?"

Chet shrugged. "The vultures are circling."

So, the farm was in trouble, and it was up to Chet to fix it. Not an easy task. When Chet turned to face her, Andrea's suspicions were proven right. His face lost the flush of excitement of showing her the inn. So, the financial difficulties were mounting. She wanted to help, but how? What did she know about running an inn? She had her work cut out for her, but she always did love a challenge. For the first time since this crazy idea of her coming on board at the inn was launched, she was beginning to believe that maybe she landed here for a reason. She turned to Chet, "You might want to consider sharing your ideas with the bank. Let them know about the new revenue sources. It may calm their concerns."

He gave her a tilt of his head and then nodded. "Would you mind if I…."

"Give them a call back?" Andrea finished his sentence. "Not at all. I'll take a walk through the rooms."

When he joined her a few minutes later, Andrea decided to change the subject. "Wow! Big room. Why all the seating?" There must've been enough for more than a dozen people in the upholstered chairs and winding sectional sprawled across the room. The oversized pillows were stacked six high in two corners and would easily accommodate another dozen.

Andrea was pleased to see Chet's face brighten with her question. "I can explain that in four simple words – the Green Bay Packers."

What is it about Wisconsin and football? She didn't get it. "Are you kidding? All *this* for football?" The words slipped off her tongue, not realizing the impact they'd have on Chet – then she remembered how he couldn't wait to get back downstairs for the playoff game yesterday at the gift opening.

His face froze. "You're not a football fan?"

Andrea lifted her shoulders. "Not really. When I was a kid, I loved how excited my dad was when he watched the games, but now I spend most weekends catching up on work or preparing for the following week. It's the only way I'll get ahead. I thought we had that in common."

"True enough, we do. But there's more to life than work. At some point, you have to take some time off and rebalance, or you'll burn out."

Andrea never considered herself on the road to burnout. She loved her job. "And watching football does that for you?"

Chet grinned. "Not just me. I suspect many of our future guests will be football fans. Everyone has a team, whether they root for them or not. Everyone knows there doesn't happen to be more loyal or devoted fans than those in Green Bay."

Andrea rolled her eyes as she walked toward the monitor. Men and their football, she mused. "Is that the reason for the big screen?"

Chet pointed out a pair of built-in speakers. "With these babies set on stadium, you'll feel as if you're right there at the game. I thought it'd be a nice offering for our guests."

Andrea took another look around the room, imagining a crowd of fans. Chet was right. A full house of football fans would fit easily in the room. Then it hit her. Of course, she thought. "Did you consider running bench seating along the long window wall?"

Chet shook his head. "Ah, no. Why do you ask?"

Andrea raised her hands. "I'm thinking you may accommodate another dozen or so fans?"

Chet nodded. "At least."

"I suspect you want a packed house? Especially for the big games and playoffs, which are happening right now, right?"

Chet stepped closer, "Where are you headed with this?

"Would you consider a cover charge?"

She could see in Chet's face he wasn't a fan of her idea.

"Hear me out. It would create another revenue stream for you."

Chet's eyes widened. "I never thought of that."

"The inn needs revenue, and you need to use every available resource. Think of it as selling tickets to the biggest game in town."

Chet nodded slowly, giving Andrea the impression he was getting more comfortable with the idea. His intentions were so pure. Chet wanted to provide a unique experience for his guests. He'd set his B&B in an elite class of accommodations. But for now, he was in trouble, and Andrea's natural inclination to help moved into autopilot.

"What about including other sports like basketball, baseball, and even the big tennis championships over the summer," Chet suggested.

He was getting used to the idea. "True. You may need another lure to get the locals up here to watch the other games."

Chet stood near the fireplace, wearing a satisfied look on his face. "I've got it. We could offer a tailgate party as we do for the football games."

Andrea frowned. She wasn't following but liked the sound of anything that could help bring money to the farm. "What's a tailgate party?"

"You've never heard of a tailgate?"

Andrea shook her head.

"Years ago, it started in the stadium parking lots. The fans would set up grills cooking brats and hamburgers. We do the same."

"It would certainly help validate the cover charge and bring in a steady stream of revenue."

Chet's eyes widened. "Andrea, that's fantastic. I'm not sure I would've thought of that myself. We make a pretty good team already, and this is only your first day.

Andrea agreed and welcomed a wave of satisfaction wash over her.

"I'll get started with finding a set of plans for the bench seating. You ready to see the upstairs?"

"I'd love to."

Chet led her into each of the six bedrooms on the second floor, each one with a private bath. Four rooms offered queen-sized four-poster beds, the other two a set of doubles. Andrea recognized the intricate handiwork of each homemade quilt folded neatly on the beds – what a lovely personal touch of comfort for each guest. It was cozy, warm, and inviting.

Andrea strolled into the last room and ran a hand across the quilt's familiar log cabin pattern. A picture flashed in her mind as she remembered the tireless hours her mother and aunt worked on their projects and the quiet conversations between them. Andrea's heart tugged in regret. Despite her mother's encouragement, she'd never had an interest in learning the craft. Now, she understood what she'd given up. It wasn't about perfecting a skill but rather about the time shared and the stories told. Maybe one day, when her career was more settled, she'd take up quilting.

She blinked away the memory, fighting an unexpected rush of emotion. *For goodness sake, what's happening here?* "Where did you find the quilts?" she asked, forcing her thoughts from nostalgia.

"Mom tells me it's a lost art. The quilts are some of her best work and the last."

"The last? Why?" It was evident to Andrea the woman had a great talent.

"It's either arthritis or carpal tunnel. Mom doesn't complain about the pain. Says she'd rather be rocking grandchildren than quilting."

Chet mentioned having a brother with kids, but now his reason for breaking up with Olivia was more apparent. It may have been the fatal blow in their relationship. There was no doubt in Andrea's mind that Chet wanted a family.

"You mentioned having a brother with kids?"

Chet nodded. "Chuck, and his wife, Kate. They have two boys, Noah and Tyler, who are eight and nine. They live down in Green Bay. Mom says she doesn't get to see the boys enough. The traffic rattles her a bit."

Andrea suspected the drive was becoming an issue for her. "Hmm, yes, I can understand, but that puts a little pressure on you, doesn't it?"

"S'pose it does." He agreed, but Andrea sensed he wasn't bothered by the expectation.

"That's the tour," Chet said as they walked side-by-side down the carpeted hallway.

"It's a lovely inn. How do you handle the guests' arrival and departure?"

"Guests check in at four p.m. and check out at eleven. I don't have much of a system in place, so I'm open to any suggestions you may have. Then, of course, there's the breakfast. It's important the guests are satisfied and plan a return trip or tell their friends about us. To be honest, the farm needs the B&B income during the off-season. I've pinned a lot of hope on this place."

"Right, the breakfast," Andrea breathed. She couldn't deny a wisp of apprehension cooking for a small crowd.

Chet gave her a look of encouragement. "You can make your aunt's waffles, pancakes, or eggs with a side of bacon."

She'd have to work close to a miracle getting breakfast on the table in a timely fashion, but wasn't she known in her family to stand up to a challenge? She certainly had a mountain-sized one in front of her now. "I can handle this."

"I have no doubt. What do you say we go down to the kitchen and find something to eat?"

He bounded down the steps like someone much younger. Andrea followed right behind him, step for step. "I love the idea. I'm famished."

"You cooking, or am I?" he asked.

"Why don't we do it together?" The words that fell out of her mouth surprised her. So far, she was enjoying herself. Her only hope was that she could pull preparing breakfast for a houseful of guests.

Chet looked over his shoulder, "Now you're talkin'."

Andrea smiled, knowing she lifted Chet out of the doldrums after the call from the bank. She only hoped they could work together and find more ways to make the inn a success.

Chapter 12

Andrea walked into the kitchen but stopped cold when her eyes focused on the oversized island. It stood its ground as if it were the lead cook in a kitchen. Spanning six feet long, its butcher-block top invited guests to run a hand along the surface before taking a seat on one of the comfy barstools on one side. She could almost hear her mother and aunt crooning over the available space to chop, roll, and whatever seasoned cooks enjoyed doing on such an expansive surface. Once again, she'd wished she had paid more attention to their work. If she had, maybe she wouldn't be in the position she was in right now – fighting a case of nerves over cooking breakfast.

Stepping toward the sink, she stole a look through the window. Evergreen trees provided shelter for red and green cardinals searching for a place to call home. Jumping from one branch to another, they rummaged for the perfect nest. It was so relaxing simply watching them. Chet had reminded her that cardinals mate for life. How beautiful they were. A rare sense of peace settled somewhere deep inside of her. Until she heard Chet calling her name, she was mesmerized by the activity.

"Hey, you're a million miles away."

Andrea folded her arms across her chest and turned to face him. He'd caught her daydreaming, yet she couldn't shake the feeling she'd made a good decision in taking the job. She was right where she was supposed to be. "I was admiring the view. You probably take that for granted, like a person who lives near the ocean but never visits the beach."

Chet shook his head. "Believe me. I don't. I've learned the hard way there's no place I'd rather be than right here."

He sounded so sure. Hoping he'd elaborate, Andrea waited. But instead, he left the kitchen and walked into the dining room, returning to the tour guide. "We tore down the wall between the dining room and the kitchen, installed new drywall on the existing walls, and put in a wood floor. After that, we painted and then brought the furniture back in."

Andrea followed him toward the expansive room. "I can see how taking the wall down opened up the space. It's beautiful." She walked toward him, recognizing the hard work that must have gone into the new room. She'd seen plenty of remodeling projects through her grandfather's trade and understood how much time and effort went into his jobs. She assumed what Chet had accomplished here was no different.

"It's a bit of a sore spot with Dad. He would've preferred to tear it down after the storm, but the insurance paid for most of the renovation, and the whole idea of a B&B came into full view. I hate to admit it, but it was a fight. I hope you can give me a few ideas for running the place. The last thing I need is more problems. I'm good with my hands, but…."

Andrea's heart melted. This big, boisterous,

confident man shared his weaknesses with her. Something inside of Andrea softened for him. She'd have to try especially hard in the kitchen. "Of course, I'll do whatever I can." The room had the same majestic windows as the projection room, with an oak table in the center. She visualized her toes working their way into the thick woolen rug, which added a hint of paisley greens and winter reds into the room. Andrea counted a dozen chairs, enough for the occupants of all six bedrooms. She imagined the guests sitting around the table waiting for breakfast. Andrea's heart began its tap-tap-tap against her chest.

Chet stood in front of the windows, wearing a puzzled look. "I couldn't figure out what to do here. Curtains? Blinds? Any suggestions?"

She looked through the windows to find mature trees tucked within a white fence running along the property lines as far as the eye could see. The sheer vastness of the great outdoors spread out like a blanket on summer grass. Soft morning sunlight streamed into the room, accentuating the mustard tones in the walls and the knots in the walnut-stained floor.

"The view is breathtaking. I wouldn't cover it up with any type of top treatment. You don't have a privacy issue, so blinds or shades are unnecessary. Look at how the sunlight perks up the room, as if sending the guests off on a positive note to start their day."

Chet ran his hand through his hair. "This is a good example of what I was trying to explain to you the other night. The place has all the basics but lacks that special something. Dad could care less, I don't have a clue, and Mom's caught up visiting my aunt in Arizona."

Chet's need for a woman's touch reached out to her.

"Let me take a guess here. You want your guests to feel as if they're home, even though they're not, right?"

"Right," Chet nodded.

"Then I'd add some extra-large pillows, a couple of throw blankets in your team colors, and keep it simple."

His smile told her they were on the same page.

She followed him back into the kitchen toward the stove.

"We have a brand-new gas cooktop with a nice griddle smack-dab in the middle, but I'm warning you, that stinker gets hot fast. Ask my fingers." He wiggled them in front of her.

Andrea giggled. She peered down at the thick steel grates of the six-burner stove and the large griddle. *Who on earth would need so many burners at one time?* She turned toward Chet. "Do you cook?"

Chet nodded, "And dance," he said, giving her a quick wink.

Andrea rolled her eyes but it was hard not to be impressed. Most men she knew were as driven as she was, leaving little room for anything else. They wouldn't think of entering a kitchen. Instead, they'd order out or insist on dinner out.

"Let me show you the freezer and pantry."

Andrea followed him into a small room off the kitchen he referred to as the back porch.

He opened one of the stainless-steel doors. Blue light illuminated stacks of frozen cherries, blueberries, and raspberries neatly labeled. Hand-rolled butter, breakfast sausages, bacon, and an assortment of juices filled the shelves.

"*This* is a lot of food. It almost reminds me of my Aunt Linda's freezer."

He nodded. "Don't be intimidated. It's here if you need it, that's all."

Andrea restrained a sigh. *He must be a mind reader.* Her eyes scanned the electrical appliances nearby. The pretty forest-green shelves were as stocked as the freezer. Onions, potatoes, and garlic sat in wicker baskets on the floor. She admitted to herself that some of the items in the pantry didn't look even vaguely familiar to her. *Great.* Now she knew she was in over her head. Then again, she was only responsible for breakfast. *Don't make it into more than what it is.* Isn't that what Chet had told her earlier?

"Oh my," she sighed.

"You can get as creative as you want with breakfast. I'll leave that decision up to you."

Creative in the kitchen. She was so out of her realm.

"I should warn you, our guests like to eat, especially if they're headed outdoors for the day, which is ninety percent of them."

Andrea moaned, remembering Chet's ferocious appetite at the wedding. She'd better plan on making a mountain of food.

"Don't worry about it. If you can survive life in the New York jungle, you can pull this off. Let's make our breakfast and get you broken in with the griddle."

He's right. She walked in the direction of the cooktop while Chet headed for the refrigerator.

"How about I crack the eggs, and you fry the bacon?" he asked.

Andrea nodded, grateful for the help. "Sounds good to me."

He handed her the package, and she turned the griddle knob to *lite.* No flame magically appeared. She heard the *clicks* of the ignitor, but that was it. *Nope! I refuse to ask for help this soon.* She felt the slight twitch of her right eye gaining strength. She cooked very little at home, now spoiled with eating out or picking up take-out. As the six-burner stove glared back at her, she realized she'd have to ask Chet for help. Before she had the chance, his hand covered hers, and her breath hitched a notch higher with his touch.

"It's a little fickle," he said, tweaking the griddle's knob a fraction from where it was.

His breath was warm and steady against her neck, pushing her heart rate up right along with the heat coming from the flame.

"Wait for the pause and the click. Then give 'er some gas."

Whoosh.

Andrea inhaled a long, cleansing breath, but it did nothing to slow her adrenaline. Chet's fingers moved with hers to shift the dial counter-clockwise to 375 degrees. She avoided his gaze, not wanting him to see his effect on her. Instead, she reached for the bacon. "Thank you."

"Tell me something. Do you live alone in the big city?" He placed a cast iron skillet on one of the burners next to the griddle and lit the flame.

Andrea stiffened. Was he asking her if there was someone special back home? "Yes, I do. How about you and Olivia? Did you live together?"

He plopped a pad of butter into the pan. "If I have the desire to live with a woman, I'll marry her first."

Andrea's eyes widened. Although progressive with his business ideas, Chet sounded a little old-fashioned. So many couples felt as if living together guaranteed a happier marriage. Andrea knew plenty of couples where the opposite had proven true. She agreed with Chet on that note. Gingerly, she placed strips of thick-cut, smoked bacon onto the griddle. The sizzle of fat meeting hot steel was immediate. "I agree with you there. No evidence living together creates a successful marriage."

"Speaking of living arrangements. You were going to tell me how you won Lila's apartment."

Grateful for the change of subject, Andrea agreed. "Oooh, that's right."

"When Lila visited Door County for a visit last October, I made a bet she'd return early, well before Christmas. The wager between us was the lease on her apartment. I was so certain she'd miss the life and energy Manhattan offers. It was all in fun. We never expected to act on it."

"I take it you won?"

"I did, but on a technicality. It all became moot after Conrad proposed."

Chet shook his head. "I don't follow."

"Lila intended on coming home early, but she was driving through blizzard conditions. She ended up in a snowbank. That's when it hit her."

"She was hit? By what, a snowplow?"

"No! Not a plow." Andrea waved the bacon tongs so fiercely to make her point the utensil flew past Chet's head and dropped onto the floor, finally sliding to a stop.

"Whoa!" Chet roared and lifted his arms as if he had to protect himself from the run-a-way utensil. "You never warned me I'd have to take cover while standing next to you in the kitchen!"

Andrea couldn't hold back her laughter. It spilled into the room like a stream of sunshine through the window. "I warned you about my cooking skills," she argued.

He handed her the tongs. "OK, go on with the story."

Andrea headed for the sink. "It wasn't a plow that hit Lila on the way to the airport. It was the truth."

"The truth?" Chet shook his head. "I'm still lost here."

A frustrated sigh escaped her as she rinsed the tongs in soapy water. *Why are men so blind about love?* She was beginning to understand why Chet couldn't find the right woman. The man was clueless. She turned to face him. "That she was in love with Conrad, and nothing was more important than that."

"Good lesson learned. There's more to life than work, isn't there, Miss Lockhart."

I certainly opened myself up to that one. "Touché, Mr. Taylor." She returned to the stove. "The story gets better. Conrad's the one that found her."

Chet let out one of his whistles, but Andrea smiled at its sound this time. She flipped on the switch for the overhead exhaust fan, clearing the air between them of cooked bacon.

"Quite a story. Is that what you hope for yourself one day? That same kind of perfect ending kind of love?"

He was pushing her again, but she didn't resist this time. Maybe the nudge was exactly the territory she needed to explore. Falling in love *again* frightened her, and she wasn't sure how to get rid of that fear. "I'm not sure I'm willing to try again after failing once already. What about you? Is there a hopeless romantic under all that rough and gruff exterior?"

"I can tell you this. I'd love what Conrad and Lila

found."

Andrea nodded. So did she one day.

After a moment, Chet asked, "How do you want your eggs? Over easy?"

"How did you know?" Andrea lifted the bacon from the pan and then slid two pieces of bread into the toaster.

"Educated guess, and it just so happens that's exactly how I like mine—runny on the plate so I can mop it up with the toast."

"I don't *mop*. Are you a butter or preserves man?"

"Preserves, preferably homemade."

"Raspberry?" she guessed.

"Oh, yeah," he sing-song replied, forcing another smile across Andrea's face.

~

After breakfast, Andrea rang the dishrag dry. "I'd like to see the project you're working on in your shop if you don't mind. You mentioned something about an antique sleigh?"

Chet put the last of the dried dishes into the cabinets while Andrea drained the sink of dishwater. "You want to do that before seeing the innkeeper's cottage?"

Andrea nodded. "I do. I shouldn't have a problem settling in."

"All right. Why don't you grab your coat, and we'll do it right now?"

They walked side-by-side toward the shop where Chet's blue pickup was parked. The December morning brought a chill that bit Andrea's nose, but the clean scent in the air caught her attention. Pure, as if a rustling spring was nearby. A light snowfall fell as they drew closer to the outdoor building. Andrea smiled at the curls of smoke snaking out of the chimney. Simple pleasures, she thought.

"That breakfast hit the spot," Chet said, breaking the silence.

"Yes, I agree. Working together made things a bit easier. Thanks for helping me out today."

"You bet. I love days that start like this one. Plenty of quiet, allowing a person to clear the mind."

Andrea surveyed the yard again, captivated by the small nuances – a train's whistle in the background, a squirrel scurrying under an evergreen. "Hmm, yes." He was right. At home, Andrea started most mornings listening to blasé news streaming from her laptop while she sipped from a mug of hot coffee. Once ready, she darted from her apartment building to the subway. This return to the great outdoors was familiar to her, grounding her.

Chet opened the shop door, and Andrea walked in ahead of him. The cold cement seeped through the soles of her new boots. Tractors with trailers took up at least half the space. An assortment of well-used oiled tools hung on pegboards lining the north wall, but the work surfaces were cluttered. It was the cobalt-blue sleigh that drew her attention. She inched closer. "It's stunning. Where did you find it?"

"Online auction. I picked it up last October in Ohio. I didn't have a chance to start working on it until now."

Andrea ran her hand over the soft upholstery, as smooth as a baby's blanket. The gold stitching had given way in the most worn sections. He'd need to replace that.

"I worked on the metal runners this morning. The front end needs a complete overhaul, and the harness hookups are rusted. There are plenty of deep body scratches that need to be filled in and buffed out. In the end, it'll need a complete paint job."

Andrea envisioned Chet in the driver's seat, offering sleigh rides across the south end of the property. "I see horse-drawn sleigh rides in the future."

Chet tap-tap-tapped the sleigh with a light hand. "You guessed it, that's the plan. I want to offer something special to our guests with Valentine's Day coming up next month. The sleigh could be a real hit."

"I hope you're considering charging for this luxury."

Chet shrugged. "I was considering it."

"Another revenue stream, Chet. Your shop reminds me of how much I loved watching my grandfather work on his woodworking projects. He had a bench in the basement. The smell of sawdust always lingered in the air." During her visits, she'd swept up the wood scraps in her grandfather's shop and returned new nails to their baby food jar containers and tools to their rightful place. Even though Chet wouldn't be working with wood, the feel was the same bringing back warm memories. "I'd love to watch the progress on the sleigh while I'm here."

Chet lifted an eyebrow. "I can always use an extra set of hands. The quicker I can get this done, the better my dad will feel about it. He thinks it's nothing but a waste of my time."

Andrea shook her head. "He doesn't see the potential as you do, but he will once it's finished. Trust me."

Chet's eyebrows rose with her suggestion. "Of course, I'll have to take it out for a run once it's up and ready."

Is he asking me to join him? She wasn't sure that would be a good idea. Starting a romance was not something Andrea should be doing. She had a new job to nail down.

"To break it in, of course," he explained and she heard the persuasiveness in his tone.

As much as Andrea wanted to glide across the lawn in a sleigh, she wasn't here to frolic away the afternoons with Chet on a horse-drawn sleigh. Without giving him an answer, she turned. "Well, I'd better get settled in and organized for tomorrow. I need to make a few calls. How's the reception?"

The easy smile fell from his face. "I'd say it's pretty good, depending on the weather. Today should be all right."

She turned for the door. "I'd better get going."

"I'll walk with you to the house and turn over the keys for the cottage. Just text me if you need anything. I'll be in the office with dad this afternoon."

"Sounds good." They walked side-by-side, returning to the quiet of the morning. Andrea assumed neither one of them wanted to fill the beautiful silence with unnecessary words. The snow crunched with each of their steps, bringing a smile to Andrea's lips. She loved the sounds of winter. A new way of life was falling into place with quiet snowfalls and early morning breakfasts. Maybe staying on in Sister Bay wouldn't be such a bad idea after all.

Chapter 13

Andrea stood on the front porch and gazed into the yard the following day. *Should I take a quick walk or not?* She shivered as the January wind picked up snow and swirled it around her legs. Instead of boarding an aircraft today, she'd prepare to welcome the first guests to Taylor Farms B&B tomorrow. She wiggled her toes in the new boots on her feet.

"You're up before the sunrise," Chet said as he rounded the corner of the house.

Andrea nearly jumped out of her new boots at the sound of his voice. She hadn't noticed anyone outside, and the pre-dawn light didn't help matters.

He raised his hands. "Hey, take it easy. It's just me."

She heard the ease in his voice as if they were old friends. "Yes, that's obvious *now*. You might consider giving a girl a little warning before sneaking up on her."

He gave her a good-morning smile making it hard to stay angry with him. "Sleep well?" he asked.

"Actually, yes. Typically, I have trouble falling asleep. I can't seem to turn off my mind. But not here."

Chet nodded. "Not surprising."

"I'm looking forward to the guests arriving later."

He rested a boot on the porch step. "Exciting, isn't

it? All the hard work that went into the renovation is finally paying off."

"I didn't see the house before you began the reconstruction, but it's amazing now. It's beautiful, Chet. I mean that."

Andrea tucked her hands into her coat pockets. She wouldn't admit to him that she was a bit anxious about cooking breakfast for a houseful of people tomorrow. They were expecting their first guests of the New Year later that afternoon. How many times had she told herself it would be a snap? Too many!

"Are you planning to stay out here?"

"Since I'm up early this morning, I thought a quick walk might be good to start the day."

"Up for some company?"

Andrea smiled noticing how well rested he looked. "Sure, why not."

He fell in line next to her. They walked down the snow-plowed driveway at a comfortable pace. "Any idea where Conrad and Lila went on their honeymoon?" he asked.

Andrea kicked at the snow as she did years ago with her little sister, Hannah, after a day of sledding. It made her feel young again. The snow slid off her boots like powdered sugar. "I don't, but I'm dying to know. All Lila shared was she had to pack summer clothes. That tells me it's somewhere warm, maybe even tropical. Did he tell you anything?"

"Nope. Besides his work on the farm, we fish together in the summer, but I don't see Conrad as much as I'd like. I can tell you his reputation is rock solid. He's made good use of his natural gifts."

"You mean with his business?"

"Yup. Hamilton Construction. He's building a legacy to pass down one day, which is what I hope to do if everything comes together. My situation is a little tough. The bank wants to send one of their realtors out to assess the place in case we need to sell. They're pushing and I'm backing away from that idea."

Andrea nodded, recognizing the connective thread between men like Conrad and Chet. Both men were building a legacy. Although Chet didn't hold the reins of the farm yet, the time she'd spent with him told her he was a born entrepreneur. The pressure of drumming up new revenue for the farm was an onerous burden. But didn't trial make you stronger? Was she stronger for what she endured? Her position on dating and falling in love again was a testimony. She'd never be a fool again. "Admirable, especially in today's economy. I think it's a lot tougher for small businesses to make a go of it. Is that what you're doing – using your natural gifts here on the farm?"

"Trying to. I wouldn't want to disappoint the man upstairs." His eyes lifted to the sky.

Andrea fell silent. His comment led straight to his faith. "Isn't it true that hanging on to your mistakes in life keeps you from moving forward?"

"Not if you're holding yourself accountable. Trading life on the farm for the card tables in Vegas was one of the biggest mistakes I made. Besides hurting my family deeply with the decision, I ran from whom I really am and everyone important to me. The worst part was I ran from God's purpose for my life. I can't change my past but I can try to fix what's broken. Some old fences still need mending."

Andrea appreciated Chet's willingness to open up on

such a sensitive topic. She was under the impression that his attractiveness on the outside was all he had to offer. How wrong she had been. What he had just shared was beautiful and came straight from the very essence of who he was. "I love the analogy. There are a few steppingstones in my life I wished I'd skipped over instead of landing on with both feet. As far as the bank goes, I'd use the power of persuasion, which you seem to have in abundance."

Chet released a laugh that made her smile. They followed the bend in the road and headed directly into the rising sun. Nearby, the birdsong of winter cardinals filled the air.

Andrea drank in the scene, mesmerized by the ball of fire inching its way over snowcapped hills. Living in the city, she'd grown used to slices of sunlight strewn between skyscrapers. Her feet slowed in front of this magnificent sunrise.

"I bet you don't see that too often."

She placed her hand over her heart. "It takes my breath away."

"That it does. God made Door County special. There's no place like it."

Lila's stories of Door County rang familiar in Andrea's ears. The one constant among the people she'd met so far was that they loved where they lived. She wasn't sure she could say the same. The big city suited her career goals, which mattered, at least all that mattered so far. "You sound like a man who's not going anywhere."

Chet gave her a half-smile. "You're right. I have practically everything I need, right here."

They were gone before she could stop the words

from leaving her mouth. "Practically?"

He tilted his head in her direction and met her eyes with his.

Andrea's stomach did that funny little hiccup.

"Almost everything," he said through a smile.

His implication was crystal clear.

That's what I get for asking. I need to mind my own business. "Right."

As they walked in the comfort of the quiet, she thought about the life she created for herself in Manhattan. There, she'd grown accustomed to the hurriedness of life. She thrived on it and forgot how healing nature's solitude was for her soul. The focus on her work had pushed everything else that was once important out of her mind. Every dream she ever had.

Chet quickened his pace on the way back to the inn. Andrea swung her arms at her sides to gain speed, forcing the cold, crisp fresh air down deep into her lungs. It was exhilarating.

Chet interrupted her thoughts. "Interested in breakfast? It would give you another trial run with the griddle."

Should she admit at least a dozen more trial runs with that beast of a cooktop would be best? They'd made bacon and eggs yesterday, and everything went well, but she needed to set a routine before the guests arrived. "Sounds good. I'm not sure what's going on, but my appetite is bigger than ever."

"It's probably the fresh air."

Andrea laughed. "The air? Please. That makes absolutely no sense."

"You don't have to believe me, but we hear it all the time from visitors. You've already admitted to sleeping better."

Andrea huffed. *He's right.* She was sleeping better, but her appetite too? She hoped he wasn't right about that.

"After you ask for second helpings, my point will be well made."

Andrea gave him a light push throwing him off the driveway's track. "You're going too far! That will never happen."

Chet chuckled. "Uh-huh, give it some time." He began a light jog, so Andrea quickened her step. It didn't take long before she was speed walking, then doing her best to run. Following Chet right off the driveway, she plowed through the snow and almost tripped. Then, she fought her way down the snow-covered path toward the house on Chet's heels, even though she knew they were acting like a couple of kids.

~

After breakfast, Chet headed for the office to work with his dad on the incoming orders, while Andrea devoted the early afternoon to the files Jim had sent her. Then, a little before three, her alarm went off, reminding her to call Jim before the guests arrived and bring him up to speed on her progress. He picked up right away.

"Andrea, glad you called. How are you getting on out there?"

A smile spread across her face. Jim made it sound like she'd moved to a remote island or the Australian Outback. "So far, so good. Thanks for the email with my accounts." She wouldn't admit that she'd only taken a glance at the numbers and then spent most of the afternoon with a new app she'd found to help out the inn. After a quick online tutorial, she implemented the program. She couldn't wait to tell Chet how much easier guest registration would be.

"Of course. I hope you found a place to stay with enough peace and quiet. Hotels can be noisy."

"I decided to take the job at the inn. I have my own cottage with plenty of room and time to devote to my work. We're expecting our first guests today. It's exciting and working out beautifully so far. How are things on your end?"

"Busy, as I expected. I thought I'd be able to wind down my career with this new position, but I'm having second thoughts with each passing day."

Relief filled her that Jim didn't challenge her decision to stay. They chatted on various topics during the call, but Andrea couldn't shake the notion that maybe it was time she took over the reins of her career. If she did, Jim would be relieved of the burden and able to focus solely on his own situation.

After the call, Andrea eased back in the desk chair and ran down the mental checklist for breakfast tomorrow. She couldn't decide what placed her in such good spirits today despite her lack of career plans. Maybe it was the fresh morning air, the quiet movements of cardinals in the trees, the utterly spectacular curtain rise of the sun, or maybe the new task of running the inn. *Maybe it's everything!* Bottom line – she was happy, in this new world that was so different than her life back home.

Chapter 14

Early Wednesday morning, Andrea muffled a yawn as she walked into the kitchen and flipped on the lights. Eight guests would expect breakfast, so she rose to tackle the job with the birds. After she clipped back her hair, the absolute first order of business was coffee. The stronger, the better. After all, it was only six a.m. She filled the reservoir with water and measured the grounds into the basket, doing her best to ignore the butterflies taking flight in the pit of her stomach. *I can do this!* She slipped the pretty floral apron over her head and headed for the refrigerator.

With the waffle recipe in hand, she searched for the cold ingredients. Finally, she found the bacon, pushing aside the half-emptied jar of spaghetti sauce, organic butter, and a package of ground beef. A blast of icy air ran across the floor with the opening of the back door. She peeked around the side of the refrigerator to find Chet stuffing his leather gloves into his coat pockets. He closed the door with a firm hand.

He lifted an eyebrow and grinned. "I thought I'd join the guests for breakfast this morning. Oh, by the way, Dad's on his way too."

Andrea knew how critical first impressions could

be, especially with a new business. *Is he checking up on me?* She was certain he was especially after telling her how important a new revenue stream was needed for the farm. Still, she wished she knew he was planning on showing up first thing this morning. She ducked her head behind the refrigerator door and tapped her cheeks with her fingertips. Regretting not getting out of bed as soon as the alarm went off, she was left with just enough time to pull herself together. She wished for a dab of pink blush to brighten her pale complexion. But instead, she pulled a few strands of her hair from the pins to frame her face, grabbed the bacon, forgot the eggs, but hooked the milk jug with a free finger and headed toward the kitchen island.

Chet stood in the doorway. He looked as if he'd just finished skiing the slopes. His heavy boots, reddened cheeks, and green and gold knit cap freckled with snow fit the illusion of a mountaineer to a tee. For a moment, Andrea wished she'd met him outside earlier for another morning walk. He looked refreshed and ready for even the most daunting tasks while she struggled to wake up this morning. He removed his coat and hat and shucked off his boots. Snowflakes flittered through the air, landing on the clean floor below. "Where do you want me?"

His question threw her. She gave him a puzzled look, but all she saw was a man rubbing his hands together, ready to dig in and get busy. *He wants to help.* "If you wouldn't mind frying the bacon that would free me to mix the waffle batter." She headed back to the refrigerator for the eggs.

"Waffles today?" The look on his face erased all the apprehension she'd felt earlier with the suggestion of a new breakfast item.

"I assume you have a waffle iron?" Then, regretting never asking the question, she returned to the island with the eggs and waited for his answer.

"I'm drawing a blank. It'd be in the red cabinet on the back porch if we had one."

If? Andrea ignored the churn in her stomach. *I should have checked last night.* She followed Chet into the back porch. She stared at the stacks of cookware and electrical appliances squeezed on the shelves in the tall cabinet next to the freezer. They pulled cake pans, flat cookie sheets, and muffin tins from their spaces and found everything except a waffle iron.

"Oh no." She tried not to sound too disappointed. She called her Aunt Linda last night specifically for the waffle recipe. It wouldn't be long before the guests would be down, expecting breakfast. There was no time to waste. *I need to think of something fast.* "Maybe I can improvise and use this recipe for pancakes."

Chet threw her a grin, wiping away her anxiety. "Pancakes taste as good as waffles to me."

He's right. Andrea refocused. She'd handled more arduous negotiations on behalf of her authors than figuring out how to manage a breakfast. "It'll have to work."

She retraced her steps back to the island, Chet now on her heels.

"I'll make the bacon in the cast iron skillet so you can use the griddle. Right after, I grab myself a cup of coffee."

"I made a pot this morning," Andrea said as she returned to the island with the eggs.

"You made coffee?"

Andrea patted herself on the back for the element of surprise. "If that's hard to believe, you'd better buckle your seatbelt because I'm about to make breakfast."

With Chet's laugh, Andrea began to relax.

"Sounds good to me. I'm starved."

Andrea remembered Chet's ferocious appetite. *I'd better triple the recipe.* As she arranged the ingredients and kitchen tools she would need for the batter, she stole a look at Chet. His large fingers struggled to reopen the seal on the bacon package. The scabbed-over scars on his hands were impossible not to notice. Her heart softened. Before giving it a second thought, she reached over and placed her hands on top of his to help. Time seemed to stop as she struggled to keep an even breath. His cologne—fresh snow and pine stampeded her senses, confusing her train of thought. "Let me help you."

"These, ah … these hands …."

Andrea slipped a polished nail between the plastic sleeves of the package. Mornings like this are what life would look like with this roll-up-your-sleeves kind of man—one who would help you complete the simplest tasks, such as frying bacon for breakfast.

"Did everyone check in last night?" he asked, walking toward the cooktop.

"All eight." Andrea stirred the batter in tornadic circles with a hand whip. "You were open to changes, so I made a few with the check-in process."

The bacon began to sizzle. "I was hoping you would."

"I downloaded a new app and had everyone use it for check-in. It will generate a monthly report if you want one. I'd encourage it because if you keep a record of your guests, you can track your high season and adjust your pricing accordingly."

Chet nodded. "Are you suggesting we raise prices because I love the sound of that? The sooner I can recoup some renovation costs, the sooner I can pay down that loan."

"You may want to down the road. I also added their time of arrival. It may be important to have that information. I'll do the same process when the guests check out."

"Either you know what you're doing, or I've hit the jackpot bringing you on board."

Andrea smiled, appreciating the compliment. It felt good to use what came naturally to her in a brand-new way. She brought the waffle ingredients together in a large stainless-steel bowl. *I should've paid closer attention.* She swirled the mixture around and hoped to recognize the right consistency even though she'd never made waffles before, much less a tripled recipe. "Any luck with your dad and the organic ideas you talked about?"

Chet cracked the eggs into a Pyrex bowl. He was taking on the task of making the eggs. "He seemed impressed after I showed him our profit margin. Thanks to you."

Andrea's eyes widened. "Me?" She poured the batter into pancake rounds on the griddle. They didn't quite look right, but she had no idea why. She couldn't remember her Aunt Linda's. But hers were taking on an unusual height. If this was her best work, she was in trouble. How would she manage this job? Tiny batter drips dribbled down the bowl's sides, splattering onto the griddle.

"If you remember, you suggested fixing a problem

with an organic solution," Chet said bringing her back on point. He lifted a few strips of bacon off the griddle and placed them onto a platter.

Andrea had trouble flipping over the monstrous cakes. They had nearly doubled in size. Something was off, but she didn't want Chet to notice. She had to come through so the inn would be a success. She'd have to bluff her way through this. "Oh! That's right. And?"

"One of our biggest problems is getting enough of the right fertilizer over the winter. An egg farm in Fish Creek started an organic fertilizer operation. I've been talking with the plant manager about buying their product. I spoke with Dad about it."

"How did he respond?"

"He said one less headache for us. So, I'm taking that as a good sign."

Andrea smiled, thrilled her idea worked out for Chet. "That's terrific."

"As I said, I've got you to thank for that idea." Now that the bacon was fried, Chet poured the beaten eggs into the pan and began to stir.

"Happy to help." When Andrea heard a few guests enter the room, she asked Chet to watch the cakes. Then, she led them to the dining room, offered them coffee from a side buffet table, and explained breakfast would be out in a few minutes.

By the time she returned to the kitchen, Chet had an egg whip in one hand and a flapjack turner in the other. His brow was dotted with tiny beads of sweat.

"Looks like you have your hands full." Andrea giggled. She took the turner from his hand and flipped the remaining cakes. The blackened edges were hard to miss.

Chet said, "We can trim those right off. No one will know, but they sure are tall, aren't they?"

Andrea stared at the griddle realizing Chet was right. Her pancakes looked odd. Was it possible she miscounted the eggs during their conversation? Or perhaps she'd used the incorrect measurement for the baking powder. Didn't that make things rise? Andrea pressed her lips together to avoid a frown spreading across her face. *More math calculations.* The subject she despised. She ignored the twitch that started up by her right eye, squeezed the last of the pancakes onto a large serving platter, and gave Chet a worried look.

Chet inhaled as he studied the platter of cakes. "I have a solution." He darted for the back porch and returned with a frozen bag of blueberries. "We'll heat this package of berries and thicken them with cornstarch and water."

Andrea exhaled. "That could work. We could spoon the berries over the pancakes to disguise the problem?"

"Right, but before we do that, let's press them down a little. That way, no one will notice."

Andrea shook her head. "I'm not sure about that."

"Believe me, as long as they taste good. We're golden, which means our patrons will spread the good news about the inn. Exactly what we need."

His simple reassurance set her fears to the sidelines. She scolded herself for thinking he was checking up on her earlier. Chet was here to help her not supervise her. "How did you learn to do all this?"

Chet quickly lifted a shoulder. "What? Make breakfast?"

Andrea turned off the burners for the griddle. "For a large group of people with relative ease despite a potential disaster? That's impressive, Chet."

He shrugged. "As a kid, we always seemed to have a small crowd around. First, it was the relatives, then friends, and now this, the B&B. But I like what I hear from you."

Andrea rolled her eyes. "I'm afraid to ask."

Chet's grin warmed the room. "Admit it. You want to know more about me."

Maybe I do! "Let's get this breakfast onto the table, shall we?"

Thirty minutes later, Andrea emptied the sink of dirty water. "Next time I make them, I'll pay more attention to the recipe."

Chet returned the last plate in the cabinet. "It all turned out, and no one suspected a thing."

Andrea was still bothered by the mishap. "I must have miscounted the eggs or added too much baking soda. They were the tallest pancakes I've ever seen, but the guests liked the blueberry sauce."

"Your idea of disguising them on the large platter and then adding a shot of whipping cream stole the show. What a sight! Even Dad whooped when we walked into the room holding that masterpiece!"

Andrea giggled. "I'm glad we managed, and I have you to thank. I'm not sure I would've gotten through it without you."

Chet bumped her shoulder with his. "I love it when you need me."

"For goodness sake!" Andrea heard the implication in his voice but realized he was right. An equal amount of interdependence between two people was healthy.

"I've got an eleven o'clock meeting in town, so I'd better run." He threw on his jacket and gear and headed out the door.

Andrea peered into the adjoining room. Everything looked to be back in order. How refreshing to have a simple sense of order and accomplishment for the day. She turned back to the sink and wrung out the dishcloth. She gazed out the kitchen window and watched Chet walk to his truck as if he had all the time in the world.

Chapter 15

Later, back at the cottage, Andrea tried working on her accounts, but her attention to detail was lost. She moved her attention to her job search but felt too far away from the action to really dig deep into the task. After she touched base with a few colleagues to inquire about any leads they knew about came up dry, she decided to turn her attention to housekeeping. Now, she paced from her living room to her kitchen. It wasn't helping.

I'll try calling Jim.

He picked up on the second ring.

"Jim, hi, it's Andrea. Have you heard anything?"

Jim's sigh rang loud and clear over the line. "Not much, kiddo. Most of the decision-makers are off on holiday break, and I might be losing a lot of my old contacts on the downside of my career. You OK?"

"I'm going crazy here thinking about facing a future jobless."

"I'll bet. You're out of the loop. Do you regret staying?"

Andrea bristled, hoping they weren't going to discuss her decision. "It doesn't make a difference whether I'm here or there. I still wouldn't know what my future looks like."

"True enough, but be sure to keep your priorities straight. I'll continue to work on my contacts. See who's hiring. Be ready to leave at a moment's notice."

Now it was her turn to sigh. The thought of leaving depressed her but she didn't want to share that with Jim. "Sounds good," she said and plopped onto the sofa in the living room.

How's the accounting coming?" Jim asked.

"Not very well. I can't seem to focus."

"Don't say I didn't warn you. You should have plenty of peace and quiet with the holidays behind us. I'm not familiar with Door County, but it sounds pretty sleepy from what you told me. It must be a ghost town with the Christmas season over."

She felt a smile light up her face. "Oh, you'd be surprised. A new ski hill has opened, attracting families to the area. With almost daily snowfalls, we're noticing snowmobilers and cross-country skiers arriving. Valentine's Day is right around the corner, and that's a huge draw for honeymooners, anniversary celebrations, or even weddings. It's not like home, but Door County is buzzing with life." She surprised herself and hoped to impress him with the number of details she'd garnered from conversations with Chet.

Jim chuckled. "You're beginning to sound like a local. Are the doldrums of the great outdoors getting to you?"

Andrea's heart softened with Jim's inability to visualize the beautiful destination she landed in. *He doesn't get it!* "That's hardly the case, Jim. There's a different order of life here. One almost opposite from ours, but dull is the last word I'd use to describe it."

"Uh-huh. It sounds like I need to let you get back to the books. If I hear anything, I'll give you a ring."

"Sounds good, Jim, thank you. I can always count on you, can't I?"

A soft chuckle reverberated over the line. "Well, we both know who I promised to do exactly that."

My dad. Andrea smiled. "Yes, we do." But, after speaking with Jim, Andrea began second-guessing her decision to extend her stay. *Is his implication right? Are my priorities mixed up?* When would she be able to make a decision and feel good? There were times she'd outgrown Jim's overseeing eye, even resented his constant advice but other times when she counted on him. She was in the middle.

Andrea peered out of the window and rubbed at her aching forehead. The brisk walk she'd taken with Chet the other day did a good job chasing away the morning jitters. The mail was probably sitting in the mailbox. *I can go pick it up.* She reached for her coat, slipped on her boots, and decided against her hat and gloves. The brisk winter air would re-invigorate her. Afterward, she'd buckle down at her desk with a cup of hot tea.

It didn't take more than a few minutes for Andrea to regret her decision not to dress for the weather. Too stubborn to return to the house, she tucked her chin behind the coat's collar and thrust her hands deep into the fur-lined pockets. Lila would be home in a few days, and they could get started on the work they had in front of them.

Walking down the plowed driveway toward the mailbox, Andrea trudged against the thick snowflakes. She retrieved the bundle of mail and turned back toward the house, now a blurry fortress ahead. The sky was heavy with gray clouds, bringing truth to the prediction of another six inches of snow by nightfall. She was beginning to understand why outdoor activities were so popular here.

As she neared the house, she noticed smoke coming from the shop's chimney. *Maybe Chet's working on the sleigh.* Fighting the wind and snow, she focused on the shop in the distance and stomped off in that direction.

~

Chet was busy working an oily rag into a wrench but was interrupted by the familiar squeak of the door. Peering over his shoulder, he saw Andrea. Her dark hair was sprinkled with snow.

The woman was breathtaking. "Hey, you."

As she walked toward him, he could tell she wasn't in a good place. Her hair was the color of black ink from the newly fallen snow, and her cheeks were as red as Door County's cherries. Still, even in disrepair, she held his heart in her grip. From her looks, she'd left the cottage without her hat, scarf, or gloves. *In this weather?* Something was on her mind. Big time. "Oh, oh. Someone's in trouble. I hope it's not me." Chet threw her a half-smile trying to lighten the moment.

She walked toward him. *It's nothing* came out like a murmur.

Right. Chet understood enough about women to discern that was the furthest thing from the truth. He laid the wrench on the steel-gray workbench and poured two cups of steaming coffee from his thermos into the camper's mugs. He handed one to her, assuming she could use it. She laid the mail on the bench and curled her fingers around the cup's warmth.

He leaned a hip against the bench and slid one boot

behind the other, giving her his full attention. "You have good timing. It's break time." *Who am I kidding?* The sooner I finish working on this sleigh, the quicker it will be available for the guests. Maybe once his dad saw another revenue stream coming in for the farm, he'd agree it had been a good move. Until then, Chet dodged the subject. Upsetting his dad wasn't high on his list, but it was up to him to make sure the payment made it to the bank on time. There were times he felt as if he were pinched in a vice.

Andrea unzipped her parka. A thick woolen sweater the color of her eyes peeked out of her coat, accentuating their beauty. He decided against filling in the silence and relied on his patience. Now was when he needed the attribute he was known for to come through. She'd come in here to talk, and he had no intention of messing that up.

"I'm second-guessing the decision I made to stay, and from the sounds of it, Jim's not thrilled about it either. I spoke with him a while ago."

Chet nodded his agreement but held back on adding his opinion. Instead, he followed her eyes to her boots. The snow had melted, creating a small pool of water on the concrete floor.

She placed her half-finished coffee on top of a metal storage cabinet. "Oh, I'm sorry. I'm making a mess. I should go."

He chuckled. "If that's the worst thing that happened today, I can't complain. You should see some of the stuff Dad drags in here without giving it a second thought. It's a shop – don't worry about it."

She folded her arms across her chest. "There are times I can't seem to make the right choice. Was staying the right decision, or should I be home conducting the job search of a lifetime?"

Chet wasn't sure how to help. "How did Jim feel about you extending your stay? Was he on board?"

She picked up her mug and looked into the black coffee as if it held the answer to his question. "He was, and he wasn't. It's been forever since my last vacation."

Chet could almost predict the answer to his next question, but he asked it anyway to make his point. "Which was?"

Andrea shrugged. "I can't remember."

"I see. And you're second-guessing your decision to stay. Why?"

"I wanted to stay after you told me your father was excited about me coming on board, and then you spoke to your Mom about me. I couldn't let your entire family down. Then Lila wanted a sit-down meeting to discuss strategy, but—"

"You're concerned about how it looks?"

Andrea winced, then nodded.

"So, you decided to stay, but now regret is seeping into the picture. Did you try praying before making your decision?"

Andrea's frustrated sigh concerned him. "I would have years ago, but I found out it doesn't always help, does it?"

Chet shot her a questioning look. "We don't always get the answers we want if that's what you mean. That's when trust moves in."

"I found relying on myself is much more predictable."

She's given up on her faith. Chet recognized the dangerous wall she'd erected. Dreams had a way of dying behind that wall. He couldn't ignore the defensiveness in her tone either, as steady as one of the support beams he'd used to build the shop.

"You want to tell me what happened that brought you to that conclusion?" He was treading in tumultuous waters now but hoped she saw the sincerity in his eyes.

Andrea sighed. "My first husband, Ben, decided to change his career track. Eventually, it destroyed our marriage and plans for a family. I prayed more than at any other time in my life. But, the end of us still came."

"That's tough." Chet nodded, not wanting to dismiss an event that changed her view of God. She must have suffered enormous pain letting go of that kind of love. He now understood another piece of her life puzzle and why this beautiful woman had entered his life became clear. He placed his mug on the bench.

"Why don't you and I make ourselves an old-fashioned pact? Let's be honest with each other from this point forward. Then maybe we can help each other out."

"May I ask you something first?"

Chet straightened. "OK, let's have it."

"Why did you leave the farm?"

Chet inhaled. The question that fell from her lips brushed over a deep wound in his heart. "I was seduced into believing I had a different destiny than the farm. I was pretty good at cards and decided, why not make a living out of it?"

Andrea's face softened. "What changed?"

"Hitting rock bottom. At that point, all I wanted was what I gave away. There are times God allows our lives to move into a trial. But it's then we learn the greatest lessons. I certainly did. God opened a door back home after my father's stroke." He knew he had touched a place deep inside her in the warm smile she gave him.

She nodded. "I think I will enjoy your idea of honesty between us."

He offered his hand, and she slipped hers in his. "Deal?" he asked.

Andrea nodded. "Deal."

Before he would have liked it, her hand fell from his, but not before an idea struck him. "Would you like to know what I do when life starts closing in on me?"

"I'm almost afraid to ask." The smile that lit up her face reminded him of the breathtaking sunrise they had shared. He had to tell himself to breathe.

He set his cup next to hers. "I get outside and have some fun. Sometimes, the best remedy is to stop thinking about a problem. How about you help me out on Saturday and come tobogganing with me?"

She shot him a no-way look that almost made him laugh out loud.

He raised his hands in defense. "No strings, and you'd be helping me out since the rest of the group are all couples. I'd stick out like a sore thumb otherwise. And I have to go. It was my idea."

Andrea crossed her arms. "I certainly don't intend to make a fool out of myself in front of your friends."

"Acquaintances, at best," he argued.

"I don't know. I haven't tobogganed in years. It's probably more like decades."

"It's like anything else. It comes right back to you." He raised both eyebrows to look hopeful. "I know you'll be busy the next couple of days, but I didn't see a new reservation until Sunday. So, Saturday is wide open."

Andrea shook her head. "I'm hoping that could change with one phone call or the click of a key on our website."

She was right. "If it does, I won't hold you to it. What have you got to lose except a few hours on Saturday afternoon on a ski hill?"

Her face lit up. "I used to love tobogganing."

Chet took that as a yes. "Everyone's meeting at one o'clock. You have snow gear?"

"Everything except snow pants. But I don't need those, do I?"

A grin spread across his face. "Oh, yeah, you'd better get a pair."

"When I finish up at the inn, I plan to meet Cassie tomorrow to see her café."

Chet rubbed his palms together. "I'd stop and pick up a pair on your way home."

"OK, if you think I need them."

Chet nodded. "You're going to love this. I guarantee it. Tell Cassie I'll be stopping in as soon as she opens her doors. She's put the time into working for Conrad these last few years in exchange for some remodeling. I'm excited to see the finished product."

Andrea zipped up her coat and grabbed the mail. "I can't believe how close-knit this community is. Does everyone know everything about everyone?"

Chet chuckled. She hit the nail on the head. "Just about," Chet grinned, "that's how we like it."

Andrea sighed, "Now that Cassie's café will be opening soon, Conrad will need a replacement."

Chet chuckled. "Sounds like you're considering applying for the job, but don't you forget about your responsibilities here."

Andrea didn't stop the smile that spread across her face. "Don't be ridiculous. I have a job search to conduct and a career to return to eventually."

The more Chet got to know Andrea, the more he hoped to change those plans.

She picked up the mail and headed for the door. "You may be right about taking my mind off of things. Thanks for listening. It helped."

"Any time." He picked up the wrench with the impression to get back to work, but his cell phone rang—*the bank.* Chet sighed. They're probably calling about the payment due in two weeks. Was this necessary? He was doing everything in his power to create revenue. Couldn't they see that? If only he could speed up the reservations or get the pole barn up and running to hold events. Something had to give soon, and his prayers remained on the inn. He had to stay focused and trust. God would see him through this. Of that, he was sure. "Hello, this is Chet Taylor speaking."

Chapter 16

The next day, Andrea stepped into Cassie's café, grateful for the warmth that welcomed her. She brushed away the dusting of snow from her coat and meandered through the restaurant. Quartz-covered counters gleamed in the afternoon sunlight. The scent of roasted coffee lingered in the air, but the sound of pots rattling in the kitchen directed Andrea's steps.

"Good morning," she sang out as she inched behind the check-out counter and stepped into the kitchen.

Cassie looked adorable in a Christmas red chef's apron. "I'm so glad you made it. I need a break!" She removed her rubber gloves, gave her hands a quick wash, and then poured two cups of coffee into cream-colored mugs.

Andrea slipped off her coat and placed it on a nearby stool. "I had to wait for the last of our guests to leave for the day before coming down."

"How is it going at the inn?" Cassie asked.

"I'm enjoying it. The guests have the most interesting stories, and they're so happy to be here. It's turning out to be a gratifying job."

"Most visitors tend to come back every year. I wouldn't be surprised if the inn ends up with repeat customers."

"I'm beginning to see why. Door County is a beautiful place to visit." Andrea scanned the room, noticing dozens of neatly stacked serving trays, snow-white sugar and creamers, and a line of professional coffee makers. "I can see by its looks that you've been busy."

"I'm working on it, but there's a reason why I asked you to stop by."

Andrea followed Cassie leaving the kitchen to one of the booths in the main dining room. On the way, Andrea stopped at the jukebox in the corner. The beautiful metallic red housing held an old-fashioned record collection. *It must be an antique.*

"I know what you're thinking. The previous owner didn't want to move it. He practically gave it away, so I thought, why not keep it? There are some notable trends in coffee shops now, and this may be one of them. Who wouldn't enjoy hearing a favorite song with coffee?"

Andrea shrugged, thinking it would be very innovative, even chic. "You can count me in."

"Chet thought you could probably help me develop a name for the café. Would you mind? He said you were the first to come to mind when I told him about my problem."

Andrea smiled and then lifted her mug. "I'm flattered he thought of me. Of course, I'd love to help in any way I can. By the way, this is fantastic." The flavor of dark chocolate was hard to miss.

"Dark Chocolate Cherry. I suspect it'll be one of my best sellers. It's from a coffee roaster down in Sturgeon Bay. I use as many local vendors as I can for my supplies. Some offered to help me with advertising, and I need all the publicity I can get."

Andrea let her thoughts wander back in time to the first breakfast she and Chet had made together and the natural camaraderie between them. "Yes, I can imagine an interdependence in small-town businesses that's rather unique. A sink-or-swim philosophy."

"Exactly. And I want to swim." Cassie lifted her mug toward Andrea, and they toasted as if holding flutes of champagne.

Andrea pulled out a small tablet and the mechanical pencil she always carried. "Let's get started on that name. What I like to do is start with some basic ideas."

"That's my problem. I have too many words in my head to settle on just one."

"Why don't you start us off and tell me the first words that come to mind when you think of coffee."

Cassie sighed. "There's coffee grounds, java, a jolt of coffee."

"Right, there's also latte, cappuccino, mocha, iced coffee." Andrea watched Cassie's eyes for the spark she'd often seen with her authors and their work. "Or you may run with something simple, perhaps a blend you prefer."

Cassie lifted her eyes over her mug, "Breakfast Blend, Columbian, Dark Black Cherry?"

Not wanting to overpower the conversation, Andrea paused. All she had to do was provide a firestorm of ideas Cassie could pick from during the process.

Cassie pushed her shoulders back, a smile broadening her face. "I've got it. How does The Perfect Cup sound?"

Andrea smiled. "It fits. Do you know why I love it? Because there's no question what people will find in your shop, and that's important."

"Then it's settled. Everything is moving forward according to plan, but I hope for the right fit for the property next door."

Andrea nodded, savoring the coffee and the conversation. "Chet told me Door County is quite the tourist spot. I can't imagine it taking long for a renter to show up and want the space."

"He's right, but it would be fantastic if that business were somewhat similar to mine so we could collaborate. Did you happen to notice the place next door when you arrived?"

Andrea rose and followed Cassie across the room. "Not really. I was so impressed with your storefront. I didn't bother looking."

Cassie opened the plantation shutters revealing a small, two-story, whitewashed brick building. The arched window frame and thick wooden doors were eye-catching. It was quaint yet beautiful at the same time. The location on the Village's main street was ideal for any business.

"There's a connecting door from my store to the one next door. Would you like to see it?"

"You have the key?" Andrea asked, sensing a bit of mystery slip into their morning.

Cassie nodded. "Follow me."

Andrea walked in Cassie's footsteps across the room. When Cassie reached for the old-fashioned skeleton key from its hiding place and slid it into the lock, the next thing Andrea heard was the *click*.

Cassie's eyes met Andrea's with a hint of mischief lingering between them. Andrea's heart picked up beats as she followed Cassie through the doorway. It led them to the middle of a large empty room. Then she spied the wooden staircase leading to a small landing on the second level. She headed in its direction.

"My realtor told me this building was sister Bay's first library and a gift shop after that. It's been vacant for a while. Too small for some businesses, too big for others," Cassie said.

"It's a beautiful space." Andrea walked across the wooden-planked floor toward the entrance, appreciating two solid wood antique doors complete with brass handles. *They look at least a hundred years old.*

Cassie opened her arms wide. "I see a bakery or bookstore here. That way, our stores could complement one another. We could even piggyback special events together."

"Oh, yes. I can see books everywhere in here." Andrea agreed, reawakening her old dream of owning a bookstore. She breathed in the scent of wood. On both sides of the room, grand mahogany shelves lined the walls in a deep espresso stain. Like Cassie, Andrea could visualize pretty-jacketed books on gardening and baking next to the latest New York Times bestseller filling the open shelves. A built-in oak desk rounded one corner in the back of the room. *That can easily be converted into a check-out counter.*

Andrea rested a hand on the newel post. "There's an air of mystery with the staircase, and the quiet tones lend themselves to snuggling into an oversized chair with a book."

"Remember the article on the lavender farm in Door County that you read on the flight? Wouldn't it be lovely on top of these bookshelves?"

"It would be a stunning combination. You really do

have the mind of a small business owner. Not only would it work, but you'd also be collaborating with another local vendor."

Cassie beamed. "I found my niche. I only hope whoever moves in shares my view so we can work together. If we can, our businesses would grow exponentially."

Andrea smiled as the floorboards creaked as she and Cassie made their way around the room, loving the sound and smell of old wood. They finished their tour by viewing the second floor, equally impressed with its nooks and crannies, which added more personality than useable space. It was easy for Andrea to see a children's library, offering books and educational games, puzzles, and lots of oversized sitting pillows in the corners.

They walked side-by-side back to the door leading to the café. "What about your plans for the future? I suspect the merger's left you in a tight spot."

Andrea shrugged. "Thanks, but it's not uncommon. My mentor is putting feelers out there for me, and I plan to start the job search as soon as I'm back home. But to be honest, I've always wanted something of my own, as you have now."

Cassie slid the key back in its place above the door. "Sounds like you and I have more in common than we realized. We're entrepreneurs in the making."

Andrea followed Cassie's lead back to the table. "I suppose you're right."

"I hope things work out for you. But in case they don't, you do have options."

Andrea didn't follow Cassie's line of thought. "What do you mean by options?"

"I'd love nothing more than to have you right here

in Sister Bay and, even better, right next door. My café and your bookstore. A match made in heaven."

Surprised to hear a hard-sell tone in Cassie's voice, Andrea gave her idea a light-hearted laugh.

"What would be the difference between landing your next job here or back home? Did you consider it may be time to switch things up? Conrad used the same argument with Lila."

It touched Andrea that Cassie was trying so hard to change her mind. "I suppose I could, but there's a big difference between why Lila relocated here and why I would." Despite Cassie's enthusiasm, Andrea pushed her suggestion aside.

Cassie refilled their mugs with a second cup of coffee from a carafe. "Choosing a name was easier than I thought it would be. I'm glad I took Chet's advice and asked you for help."

The sound of Chet's name caused Andrea to pause. It was touching he'd recommended her. It meant he respected her decisions. "He wanted me to tell you he'll be one of your first customers when you open. He's been more than helpful at the inn, considering I don't cook."

Cassie's eyes widened. "You don't cook. You're kidding. How did you manage to end up with a job serving breakfast?"

Andrea shook her head, not believing it herself. "It was all Lila's idea."

"Lila has a hidden talent for pulling people together like her Aunt Cathy. We all ached for Conrad when they broke up but were amazed at how God brought them back together."

Andrea was beginning to agree that Lila did have a way of bringing people together. However, she wasn't sure if God had a part in her reconciliation with Conrad or if it was coincidental.

"How long are you staying?" Cassie asked.

"Until sometime next week. The office is closed for the holiday season. Lila asked for a little help getting her new series off the ground."

"Have you fallen in love with Door County yet?"

"The quiet time at the farm gives me the chance to unwind and think about my next move in my career."

Cassie slid the plastic wrap off a small plate of scones she'd brought to the table, telling Andrea she had the time to talk.

"Lately, I feel pulled in two different directions."

Cassie leaned in, "What do you mean?"

Andrea sipped from her mug and then answered. "I love what I do, and I'll probably be able to land another position, but when I notice the soft tones in the kitchen at the inn and the lovely quilts on the beds upstairs, it reminds me of all the dreams I used to have for my life."

Cassie had a look of surprise on her face. "Are we talking about a family?"

Andrea nodded. "After my divorce, I buried my dreams for children. I had to get through the pain. So, I decided to devote everything to my career and work hard. I certainly didn't plan on falling in love again any time soon, but the clock is ticking if I want a family."

"Sounds like you and Lila have more to talk about than her new series."

Andrea nodded, pleased she finally admitted to what she'd been feeling the past few days.

"I wish I could give you some good advice, but I'm still waiting for the right guy to walk into my life. Unfortunately, I haven't been the luckiest in love either."

Andrea gave her a warm smile. "And the right man may walk right into your café any day now. I mean that literally. Chet told me how Lila and Conrad reconnected. In the back of the store at Window Shopping. The same could easily happen here."

Cassie rolled her eyes. Unlikely. "I'm not sure there's a man alive that'll pass the marks on Conrad's checklist."

"Big brother at work, huh? That's too cute, and you know it." *What about Chet?* He was successful, attractive, and taking action to correct the mistakes he'd made in the past. Certainly, Conrad wouldn't object to Cassie dating *him*. Andrea couldn't put the brakes on her curiosity. "Chet is an interesting man."

"He is, but we tried and found out years ago, that we're not a good fit. Friends, yes, but that's it, which is too bad because Conrad gave me a thumbs-up, which says a lot. But no, Chet's like a big brother to me."

Interesting. Andrea's phone alarm whistled its tune. "I wish I could talk more, but I'd better get going. Chet's invited me to a toboggan party on Saturday. He strongly advised I pick up a pair of snow bibs."

Cassie chuckled. "Oh boy, I've heard plenty about those runs. Are you going to the new hill? I've heard it's as fun as Little Sweden used to be."

Andrea slipped on her coat. "I guess so. Wish me luck. I was fourteen the last time I was on the back of a toboggan."

"Be prepared for the unexpected," Cassie warned, wearing a grin.

What does she mean by that? Before walking out the door, Andrea asked, "Should I be concerned?"

"If I know Chet, he'll take you by complete surprise.

The man seems to be a genius at it."

"I'm finding that out day by day. See you later, Cassie, and thanks for the coffee."

"Thanks for the brainstorming session. It helped."

Andrea moved quickly down the street toward the local outfitting store in pursuit of a pretty pair of outdoor bibs. The last thing on her mind was conducting a job search or the accounting work that waited for her back at the inn. *I hope I can handle the unexpected!*

Chapter 17

After a quick breakfast, Andrea joined Chet in his truck to ride over to the ski hill on Saturday morning. She steered her gaze out the window and allowed her lids to close. The remaining guests checked out of the inn yesterday, with more expected next week.

As they drove up the narrow road leading to the hill, Andrea was pleased with how the first week at the inn had gone. She wouldn't call herself a natural in the kitchen, but her system for breakfast was down, and she was still coming up with small innovative management ideas.

She was disappointed in her lack of discipline with her accounting and her disinterest in her job search. She intended to do a better job but couldn't shake the feeling that her priorities had changed. She enjoyed improving the guest registration process or running brand-new marketing ideas for the inn past Chet. The best part was that he was open and willing to try them to make the inn work. Andrea couldn't shake the desperateness in his tone, so she kept her mind busy with more strategies and opportunities to spread the news of the inn. Some of their conversations segued over to the pole barn and all the possibilities to come offering it as a banquet hall or meeting venue.

As Chet turned toward the hill, Andrea tugged at the insulated white bibs she wore over her jeans and sweater. She should have waited until they reached the ski hill to put them on. She was roasting.

Chet glanced at her. "You look fine. Quit your fidgeting."

"I don't remember bibs being this uncomfortable. I feel like the doughboy on the refrigerated biscuit can!"

Chet chuckled. "Everyone else will look the same, including me." He patted his midsection.

"Somehow, I don't agree." She looked at him with different eyes realizing they complemented each other in a striking kind of way.

He pulled into the already jammed parking lot, pulling Andrea from her speculation. He slid the truck into the first available space and cut the engine. "Whoa, looks like a full house today."

The few stalls left implied the whole village decided to join them, but it was a perfect day for the slopes. "I had no idea so many people would be here." Andrea met Chet at the back of the truck. He lowered the tailgate, then leaned into the bed, reaching for the rope of his sled. That's when she saw it, *Alley Cat*. "You gave your toboggan a name?" She asked through a giggle.

Chet puffed out his chest and lifted his shoulders. For a split second, the extra fabric in the bibs he wore transformed him into an adorable Santa.

He laid the toboggan on the ground next to them and flipped up the tailgate while Andrea hid a smile. "Naming the sleds makes it a lot easier for the races."

"Races?" Andrea shrieked. *Oh, no!* She couldn't remember the last time she'd tobogganed, and now he was expecting her to race? She hoped she misunderstood. Instead, she heard Cassie's warning in her head about Chet's special gift for the unexpected.

Chet shot her a questioning look. "I thought I told you," he winked.

Uh-oh. Told me? The man was as unpredictable as the weather. "No, you didn't! You made it sound like a couple of toboggan runs with a few friends. You didn't say anything about racing."

Chet grinned and walked up the hill toward the crowd, pulling the sled behind him. "It'll be fun. We decided to beef it up a little bit with some noncompetitive races. Trust me."

She stomped like a reluctant child before hurrying to catch up to him. "You do know you used an oxymoron, right?"

"An oxy what?" he asked as he scanned the crowd, searching for his friends.

She was about to explain it to him when a man dressed in a metallic gray snowmobile suit approached Chet. Andrea read *Pete's Garage* logoed onto the upper right corner. Pete's wind-swept hair and unshaven face gave a Viking-like impression, and the scowl on his face told Andrea he meant business. She inched closer to Chet, fighting the impulse to run.

Andrea held her breath when the snowmobile-suited man stopped dead in front of Chet. He dug his army boots into the snow, turning the white powder into two dark ruts like a bull. *Oh, no, this isn't good.* Before she could ask the question, Chet thrust forward and placed his hands on the brute's shoulders, dropping the toboggans rope. His opponent lunged for Chet's legs.

Andrea grabbed the rope when the sleigh slipped

back down the hill, catching it just in time. The onlookers began to pool around the men nudging each other to get a good view. *Why isn't anyone else as afraid as I am?* Then, to her utter amazement, a chant began. "Fight Ben, fight. Turn him over, now!"

Andrea froze. She squeezed the rope until it caused her to wince, then loosened her grip. She looked at the good-sized crowd encircling the men. Everyone else seemed to be enjoying the brawl. *Should I run for help?* She scanned the area looking for a lifeguard as if they were on a beach with help only a shout away. Prickles of frustration nibbled at her neck as her heart pounded in her ears. She was so out of her comfort zone.

The crowd backed up, giving the two brawlers enough room to roll from side to side. Grunts and groans filled the air. Then, *thump!* Someone's back hit the ground—hard. Andrea squeezed her eyes shut. *Don't let it be Chet!* Through squinted eyes, she found Ben squirming under Chet's boot on his chest, but the relief that filled her was temporary. Her imagination saw Ben breaking free and tackling Chet for a second round. *What have I managed to get myself into?*

Ben did his best to worm his way out of his predicament, but Chet's quick responses gave him a foothold over his opponent. Secretly, Andrea wished he'd back off so they could make a run for it. What on earth was he doing? Chet's laugh both released the tension in her body and infuriated her at that same time. He was enjoying this! Cassie's warning echoed in her head, 'If I know Chet, he'll take you by complete and utter surprise.'

"Had enough?" Chet hollered.

"I'll get you next time. Now give me a hand," Ben

demanded. As soon as he got back on his feet, he rammed his shoulder into Chet's. "Fair fight."

Chet could have told me this was coming. She was fighting a good dose of agitation and then noticed Chet's eyes searching for her through the crowd. When their eyes met, a broad smile slid across his face. It melted her anger like the sun shining down on the ski hill right now. After repositioning the knit cap on his head, Chet parted the crowd, walking straight for her. "Hey everyone, say hello to Andrea. She's riding as my second today."

Andrea smiled. The anger that filled her a moment ago now slipped off her shoulders like new falling snow. That smile Chet just gave her when he'd introduced her told her how happy he was to find her still here. It was impossible to stay angry with him now.

Thirty minutes later, Andrea and Chet stood with five other teams listening to the instructions for the race. She couldn't believe she agreed to do this, but Chet convinced her it was all in fun.

Jake, the organizer for the day, brought the small crowd together with a loud whistle. "We've got six teams today: Alley Cat, Dead Eyes, Curiosity Bites, Black Tales, Howling Wolf, and Snake Eyes. Of course, we all know the rules: keep your limbs inside, no standing on the sleds, and shove off as soon as you hear the whistle."

Andrea lowered her voice. "Standing on the sleds?" She'd never heard of anything so ridiculous, not to mention dangerous.

Chet nodded, "Some claim it's an advantage in steering, but you pull that, and you're automatically disqualified."

This race is serious! Andrea couldn't deny the excitement building as she followed Chet over to Alley

Cat. She watched as the sledders positioned their toboggans behind a yellow nylon rope. Its frayed edges told Andrea it had been a part of too many runs as it stretched across the competitors, preventing false starts.

"You ready?" Chet asked, drawing her under his arm.

"All set, but you'll have to tell me what to do here." She heard the anxious excitement in her voice.

"OK, I'll take the lead, and you sit right behind me. Move with my body weight so we can use it as an advantage. Hang on tight. Some of the sledders like to get a little too close. There's always an opportunity for dirty play, especially when we're flying down the hill."

Andrea cringed. "I see bumper cars in my head." She opened her eyes wide to accentuate her point.

"Yup, that's about right. Hang on to me, tight, and you'll be OK."

Great! This race was not only competitive, but it also had the potential to turn physical. In frustration, she picked up a mound of snow and threw it right at Chet. It landed smack dab in the unprotected spot at the back of his neck. *Good, a direct hit.*

Chet arched his back in protest. "Ah!"

The final whistle shrilled its tune, preventing Chet's retaliation. Chet and Andrea lunged for Alley Cat, pushed off, and careened down the hill. Andrea screamed as they soared down the steep slope, holding on to Chet for dear life.

~

Chet had difficulty believing how fast the time had gone when the sun began its descent later that afternoon. Today, the last thing on his mind was winning. Andrea's screams and laughs told him all he needed to know. She enjoyed the afternoon, and he'd succeeded in getting her mind off the job search ahead of her. It didn't take long before her old tobogganing skills came back. Before long, she leaned with him directing the sled to ward off the close calls as they flew down the hill. How long had it been since she'd spent an afternoon letting go and enjoying herself? From what she'd told him about how she spent her weekends, he was willing to bet it had been years. It sounded as if she strove to do her job to the best of her abilities, which Chet found admirable. In a way, they had that attribute in common.

They had one run left before losing the day to the setting sun. Chet surveyed their new position at the starting line. An alternative route quickly came into view. *The last big run.* He couldn't wait to see the look on Andrea's face when they pulled it off. "Follow my lead on this one. I have an idea."

When she gave him the nod, he had the green light to implement his plan. The whistle blew, and they took off. Chet leaned all of his body weight to the right side of the sled. Andrea was quick to follow. If the shortcut worked, they'd whiz around a cluster of arborvitaes and hit the finish line first. Maybe they could win this one. He knew they needed to pick up speed, so he crouched down as low as possible so his body wouldn't act as a shield slowing them down. Everything turned out exactly as he'd planned until the one thing Chet hadn't counted on showed up in spades.

"Ice," Chet yelled. The words flew from his lips when he lost all control. They tumbled off the toboggan, rolling in opposite directions, while their competitors hooted and hollered and roared past them down to the finish line. Alley Cat followed the group as if a traitor until getting hung up by a large branch in its path.

Chet rolled over. His first thoughts raced to Andrea. *Please don't let her be hurt.* He shimmied on his knees and elbows and found her lying on her back. She didn't look well. *Is she knocked out cold?*

"Hey, you hurt?" he asked. "I'm so sorry. I had no idea there was ice on the other side of those bushes."

"No," she giggled. "It was a perfect way to end the day. Did you plan that on purpose?"

His heart stopped when she rolled over to face him. Her cheeks, now a deep rosy pink, reflected an afternoon spent outside on the hill. Her violet-blue eyes sparkled in the last rays of the sun. *Thank you, God.* He drew closer and gently wiped the snow off her face. Sheer instinct moved him closer, his lips almost touching hers, when the sound of heavy footsteps stopped within eyeshot. Reluctantly, Chet dragged his eyes from Andrea to the man standing above them.

Jake stared down at them. "Hey, you two all right? I saw the wipeout. We've got Alley Cat."

Chet rolled over onto his back and got to his feet. He extended a hand to Andrea. "We hit the ice, and that was it for us," Chet said, wishing he'd had more time before Jake's arrival.

"That's what friends are for. Glad to see you're not hurt. Good run today."

Chet shot a glance at Jake wishing at that moment he wasn't such a good friend. *I could've kissed her!* "Remember, I've got a cookout lined up at the farm. So, we can grill out and figure out the winners."

"Sounds good to me. I'm as hungry as a horse," Jake said.

"See you at my place," Chet said. Once inside the

truck, he turned to Andrea. "Did you have fun?" he asked her once they were alone.

Andrea gave him a smile that grabbed his heart and squeezed. *Oh man, I'm in trouble.*

~

It was close to seven o'clock when Chet placed the grilled steaks onto a large platter. The group was seated on wooden benches encircling the enormous fire pit. Conrad's idea was to make the benches from the scrap lumber when they'd finished the greenhouses. At the time, Chet wanted nothing more than to be finished with the job, but Conrad insisted he'd appreciate them down the road. He was right. It had taken some time, but now Chet realized why Conrad was as successful as he was in his business. It was times like that one when Chet realized Conrad was so much more than a buddy. He was a mentor as well.

Chet tossed a few logs onto the fire. The flames licked the grill grates clean for the steaks while providing enough warmth for jackets and caps to fall to the wayside. Foil packets of French buttered bread and a side of camp-fired baked beans would finish off the meal. Simple and satisfying, the way Chet liked it. In fact, it was nights like this one he loved the most.

He took a quick look around him, realizing what a lucky man he was. Coming home was the best decision he'd ever made. The years he wasted in Nevada proved to be the most challenging lessons he'd ever learned. He was flat-out stupid, idiotic, and immature. Did he think because he was considered the *big fish* in college, he'd be one in Vegas? Right. The players out there turned him into fish bait. Man did he prove himself wrong on that one, and he'd hurt his father. Deeply. He could thank his brother for tracking him down and God, who never lifted His hand off of his life. If that meant he'd work the farm as a hand for the rest of his life, he'd do it. He deserved nothing more than the second chance his father had given him. His ideas and vision for the farm could wait.

As he continued to scan the group, his eyes rested on Andrea. Snuggled between Ben and his wife, Katie, she looked content. Happy. Earlier, he'd felt her body close in next to him when Ben approached wearing the look of a warrior as if to protect him. It was adorable. Their impromptu wrestling matches acted as an ice breaker for the group. It was all fun, but Andrea didn't know that. Maybe he should've prepared her, but he wasn't sure Ben would show. Still, the look of concern in her eyes had moved a mountain inside him. *She cares.*

There was no denying the magnetic pull toward her when she walked into his life. He could almost touch the place deep inside of her that told him she wanted the same things in life that he did, a home to share and children to raise.

Chet continued to make his way around his friends, sliding a grilled steak onto each plate, but what he couldn't do was clear his head. Andrea Lockhart had warmed a place in his heart. A place no other woman had managed to find. He hoped he filled that same special place in her heart waiting for him. Her eyes caught his. By instinct, he shot her a wink, and then he remembered where he needed to place his trust, not in himself or Andrea but in God. Only then would his life turn in the direction it was meant to go.

Chapter 18

The first image that popped into Andrea's head when she opened her eyes on Sunday morning was Chet's *almost* kiss. She brought her fingers to her mouth. She wouldn't have stopped him. *What am I thinking?* As if wiping out on the toboggan wasn't enough excitement.

She forced her feet to the floor and her body out from under the warm quilt. She shivered as she slipped on her robe and slippers and headed for the coffee maker. A good strong cup of java would help clear her thoughts and steer her mind in the right direction.

After filling her cup for the second time, she glanced at the clock and reminded herself to get moving. She'd accepted Chet's invitation to join him and his dad for Sunday service, and she didn't want to run late.

Later that morning, Andrea found herself sitting between Mike and Chet on the bench seat of Chet's truck after church. She watched Chet grip the steering wheel and barrel down the driveway toward the inn. *Why the hurry? The new guests wouldn't arrive for a couple of hours.* Snow flew up and onto the front hood hitting the windshield. Andrea gave Mike a sideways glance, but he seemed oblivious to the tension in the cab. "Chet, is everything all right?" Andrea asked.

He jerked his head in her direction. "With me? Everything's great, but we need to get a move on to get everything ready for the tailgate."

"He's right," Michael added, "playoff game starts at noon. We need to get that barbequed beef out of the fridge and into the oven. You never brought the gear down from upstairs either."

"I know, Dad. We'll make it." Chet sounded irritated. His foot hit the brakes.

Andrea braced for the stop just in time to watch the truck slide on the ice-covered snow and back into its original spot on the driveway.

Chet cut the engine. Both men opened the vehicle doors simultaneously. They were out of the truck and onto the walk leading to the house.

Andrea climbed down from the truck slamming the door behind her. She followed behind them with less enthusiasm. At least she'd have the afternoon free to welcome the new guests and maybe tackle some bookkeeping. "I didn't realize there was a game today. I'll probably stay busy with our new arrivals and then work on my bookkeeping."

Chet and Mike stopped dead in their tracks. They whirled around to face her, both wearing a look of disbelief as if she'd just announced the game was canceled.

"What?" she asked, taking a step back from both of them.

"We need every hand on deck to pull this off," Chet said, his tone serious. "Nine times out of ten, the new guests will want to watch the game along with us."

Mike nodded. Gone was the generous smile he usually gave her from ear to ear. Instead, his face now wore an apology. "He's right, kid. You're part of the team now."

Andrea sighed. "But, I don't know anything about throwing a football tailgate party."

The two men resumed their rapid pace toward the door as if she hadn't uttered a word. It was Chet who spoke first. "We talked about it on your first day. Plus, you watched the games with your dad when you were a kid. He must've had snacks. That's all this is. Just a little more."

To Andrea's surprise, preparing the tailgate went smoothly for the next hour. She worked side-by-side with the men sliding barbequed beef, a hot potato salad, and crazy beans into the oven. They were all dishes Chet had picked up from the deli while Andrea visited Cassie. Then, after straightening up the TV room, they asked Andrea to assemble a cheese and sausage platter, a bowl of potato chips with onion dip, and liver spread with rye crackers.

Andrea was about to retreat to her cottage when Chet returned to the room with a green and gold container. When Chet tossed the cover to the side, her curiosity was piqued. She moved closer and peered inside. Football coasters, extra-large paper plates, napkins stamped with a green *G*, and plastic cutlery filled the tub. But when Chet lifted a rhinestone-studded pink-and-white jersey from the bin, she wondered how far he planned to take this.

"I thought you might enjoy wearing this while we watch the game."

Watch the game? He's not serious. But the look in his eyes changed everything.

"I picked it up the other day after stopping at the

deli. I was on my way home and noticed it in one of the store windows. Your name was written all over it."

Andrea smiled, moved by his thoughtfulness. "Really? Because I don't see my name anywhere on that shirt."

"Jersey," Chet corrected, "a coveted article of clothing in these parts."

"My mistake," Andrea confessed. "Jersey," she repeated. There was no way she could refuse him now. Was it because he thought of her while running errands? Or because the jersey had reminded him of her when he was shopping? Or the vulnerability in his eyes at that exact moment? "That's incredibly thoughtful, Chet. Thank you."

"It was nothing. I-uh-I bought a small."

Andrea accepted the gift. "It looks perfect."

"Here, let me help you with that." He slipped the jersey over her head, bringing down the sides of the shirt to fall at her hips—a perfect fit. "I was right," he beamed, the look in his eyes reminding Andrea of the same tenderness that passed between Lila and Conrad at their wedding.

Life with Chet. It wasn't the first time that thought came into her mind, but why was she even going there? She had a job search to conduct. A career was waiting for her back home. Yet, the moment touched her in a way she thought had long grown cold. He cared. She stretched out her arms and twirled around in her new glittery jersey, feeling more a part of the team than ever.

Mike turned from the sink and gave Andrea a thumbs up, "Now we're talking. You're officially one of us," he grinned. Andrea and Chet chuckled along with Michael, but the moment was soon interrupted by a loud banging on the back door, causing the panes of glass to rattle in its frame.

Andrea followed Chet and Michael's gaze as they turned in the direction of the commotion. Lila and Conrad's faces peered into the kitchen.

Chapter 19

The suspicion on Lila's face caused Andrea's feet to slow. She was caught dancing around in Chet's kitchen. Andrea stepped toward the newlywed couple after Michael welcomed them into the room.

"I'm happy to see you two made it before the other guests arrived," Michael said.

Conrad strode into the room. "We flew in last night and had no intention of missing the playoff game."

Andrea walked toward Lila. She gave her friend a tight squeeze. "You smell like the beach."

Lila laughed. "You would, too, if you were rubbed down with coconut oil every day of the week."

"That a boy," Chet grinned and gave Conrad a playful slap on the back.

Mike winked at Andrea. "Come on, guys, let's give the ladies some privacy." He steered the men into the living room, where the pregame show had already started.

Grateful for the reprieve, Andrea took Lila's coat and scarf to the back porch and hung them on the coat rack.

"Did we interrupt something here?"

Andrea giggled. "I'll fill you in, but first, I have to

know. Was it an island get-a-way?" She was dying to hear all the details of Lila's honeymoon. Over the past week, she often thought how romantic it was of Conrad to sweep Lila off her feet.

"I had no idea where we were going until we arrived at the terminal. Conrad's lips were sealed. I couldn't get a word out of him as hard as I tried."

Lila still looks like the picture-perfect bride. "What a romantic!" Andrea gushed.

"He took me to the Bahamas. We flew straight into Nassau and spent the week at the Baha Resort. We had beautiful warm sunny days and walked the beach at night. I even learned how to paddleboard."

"I've always wanted to do that but never took the time."

"And I bet I know why. For years, your focus has been on your work. I'm so glad I convinced you to stay longer. Maybe this reprieve has done you some good. There's more to life, you know."

Andrea heard Chet's message ring familiar with Lila's advice. She'd been so out of balance the past ten years. Maybe it was time for a change. The time in Door County had nourished her soul and recharged her priorities. All the rumors she'd heard about Door County were true. It was a special place in the world. "Tell me more about your honeymoon. I may never get the experience at this rate."

Lila rolled a pair of don't be ridiculous eyes in Andrea's direction. "We treated ourselves to bride-and-groom massages in the afternoons and dinner on our private patio in the evening. Conrad kept it simple, yet it was divine at the same time. Does that even make sense?"

"Ahh," Andrea moaned. "I'm so jealous."

"Watching the sun melt into the ocean at sunset, Andrea, all I can say is that it was magical. Conrad thought of everything. I love him all the more for it."

Andrea remembered the sunrise she and Chet shared. "Your honeymoon sounds as perfect as your wedding. I love that he kept your destination a secret for as long as possible."

Lila nodded toward the men. "Believe me. I will never forget how close I came to missing out on a second chance for love. Of course, we both wish it wouldn't have taken so long to figure out, but God has His timetable."

Listening to her friend, Andrea was reminded of their conversations back in New York about love and Lila's faith and how their futures might unfold. Lila had reminded her more than once that nothing happened by accident. Even the years she spent apart from Conrad had brought the truth that they belonged together.

Lila's eyes widened. "Enough about me. What was going on in here when we arrived?"

Andrea took a step back from her friend, allowing a better view of the T-shirt Chet had given her. "Are you referring to the jersey Chet bought me for game day?"

Lila's eyes widened. "Wait a minute. Are you in football attire?"

"Chet said he noticed it in one of the stores and thought of me."

Lila raised her eyebrows. "He did, huh?"

Andrea took a seat across from Lila at the table. She brought her coffee mug to her lips and enjoyed the flavor of the dark roast she had purchased from Cassie.

"You look better than I've ever seen you. Rested."

Lila said. "I'm not used to seeing you like this. Our lives in New York often had both of us constantly charged. It's a refreshing change."

"Chet would tell you it comes from living in the great outdoors. He claims the air helps me sleep at night." Andrea laughed, still unconvinced of his opinion, even though she fell sound asleep most nights as soon as her head hit the pillow.

"And there is some truth to that. As much as I loved our honeymoon, I'm glad to be home again. It's where I feel the most grounded."

Andrea now shared Lila's opinion. Even though she missed the hustle and bustle of her life back home, she may never have known this new well-being if she hadn't extended her stay. "Will you miss your old life?"

Lila nodded, "I'm sure, but I'm willing to give it all up for what I have now. A brand-new chapter in my life has opened up, and I'm ready for it. Besides, Aunt Cathy is thrilled that I'm coming home. She's counting the days until grandchildren arrive."

For Lila, life with Conrad meant having a family. Chet's words rang through her head, comparing her to Lila and his prediction of children coming for them soon. At thirty-four years old, Andrea contemplated if she'd ever know that feeling, ever have the news to share with her husband that they were expecting a child. Was it regret that pulled at her heart? She understood Lila's perspective now more than ever. The past week had opened her eyes to the new life her friend would walk into, one so different than the one waiting for Andrea back home. She refilled their cups with fresh coffee, eager to continue their conversation.

Lila thanked her and asked, "How did it go last

week? A job as an innkeeper in Door County is a bit different from what you're used to in the city."

It was moments like this one that Andrea would miss the most. The one-on-one time that she shared with her good friend. "There was an adjustment period. If I told you it was full of surprises, would you believe me?"

Lila giggled. "I was counting on you two hitting it off, eventually. Knowing you as well as I do, I'm sure you've made some improvements."

Andrea smiled, realizing Lila's insight was accurate. "I managed to create a new system for guest registration, and I can cook a decent breakfast for a full table of guests. I even fine-tuned my tobogganing skills."

Lila inched forward on her chair. "Tobogganing?"

Andrea didn't stop the smile on her face as she described the afternoon on the ski hill.

"Aren't you leaving a little something out?" Lila asked.

She already knows! Andrea felt the heat creep up her neck and color her cheeks. She'd left out the most important event of that afternoon. "You mean...."

Lila nodded. "You may have forgotten Jake works for Conrad. As soon as we got home, Conrad touched base with him on how the week had gone in his absence."

"I see, and Jake filled in Conrad on what almost happened between Chet and me?"

Lila nodded. "He did. I think you have some explaining to do."

Andrea's flush grew hotter. "Lila, it was nothing. We had just wiped out and got caught up in the moment. That's all."

Lila's gentle smile widened. "Andrea, as a reader of romance, you should know that's how something wonderful usually starts. An innocent moment has a way of turning into something beautiful."

"True enough in the world of fiction, but I hope you're not implying I should apply that theory to my own life." Andrea had no intention of turning her world upside down, despite how much her heart skipped beats when she thought of Chet's lips on hers. It was a fluke and nothing more. "What I need to be focusing on now is buckling down and getting busy with the accounting work and then a gigantic job search. Jim was kind enough to send me my files, but I've made little progress since arriving. And don't forget we need to schedule some time together to work out whatever problems you've encountered."

Lila nodded. "Okay, I get it. You don't want to talk about Chet, but this conversation is not over. I'm ready to buckle down and get back to work. Maybe we'll have enough time to talk about the marketing end too. I haven't been assigned a new agent yet."

Andrea nodded, "I've already put some ideas down on paper for you."

"What will I do without you? I hate this merger."

Andrea smiled, but there were no words of comfort she could offer. Her job as Lila's literary agent had come to an end, but she planned to enjoy the last meeting they'd have, and their friendship would go on."

Conrad stepped into the room, wearing a broad smile. "Ladies, are you ready for the game?"

Lila rose to her feet and straightened her shoulders showing off her Packer's jersey. "Dressed and ready to go," she smiled.

"So am I," Andrea added, pulling back her own shoulders for a good view of her new top. She walked arm-in-arm with Lila toward the party in the other room.

~

Shortly before half-time, Chet gave Andrea a nod to meet him in the kitchen.

She felt the warmth of his hand on the small of her back. They casually walked into the next room. "Would you mind helping me get the food out for everyone?"

"Not at all. We're not a bad team in the kitchen."

Chet chuckled. "Or on the ski hill."

Andrea smiled, remembering the afternoon on the toboggan. She tied an apron around her waist, wondering how the day might have ended if they weren't interrupted. She wished Chet would've kissed her. "I had more fun that day than I thought I would."

Chet grabbed a pair of hot pads from the drawer and slid the tray of barbequed beef out of the oven while Andrea reached for the trivet. "Don't forget we won a prize for our efforts."

"Yes, the *Pair Who Tried the Hardest*. I guess that's something," Andrea giggled as she fished through the utensil drawer for the serving fork.

"Of course, it is. Next time we'll—"

Conrad strode into the room using a voice as big as his personality. "Hey, what's the hold-up on the food? They don't feed you on planes like they used to. I've been hungry since yesterday."

"We're only two people working here," Chet ribbed. "Why don't you lend a hand instead of complaining?"

"I'll get out the cold casseroles," Andrea offered.

Conrad walked alongside Andrea toward the refrigerator ready to help. "I've been meaning to thank you for helping Cassie. She told me how you came through for her and helped her figure out a name for the place."

Andrea was touched. Cassie had told her how her big brother watched over her regarding the men she dated. Here is another example of his care for her. "It was my pleasure. I have a lot of respect for young entrepreneurs like your sister. We have more in common than we thought."

"Like?" Conrad asked.

"Similar to Cassie's café, I hope to have my own little business one day."

Conrad's eyes widened. "Here in Sister Bay?"

Andrea stopped midway to the island with a casserole in hand. "No, back home, of course."

Behind her, Chet slammed the oven door moving Conrad's attention to the other side of the room. "Don't close too many doors before you know what's on the other side," Conrad said.

Andrea nodded not sure his counsel fit her life. "Thank you, Conrad, that's good advice."

He turned toward Chet. "Okay, man, what can I do?"

"Grab the beans off the stove and put them on the table. Andrea has trivets waiting for the hot food," Chet directed.

Andrea worked alongside Chet and Conrad for the next several minutes, placing platters, bowls, and trays of hot food filling every dining table space. Andrea smiled as she thought of Conrad's counsel, not to be too quick to close a door before careful consideration. Of course, she wasn't sure it applied to her. Her future had a predictable outcome. She'd tuck away his advice just in case.

Chapter 20

Hours later, Andrea returned dishes to their cabinets when she noticed an attractive woman in the next room talking to Chet. Her hands slowed. *I didn't see her earlier.* It didn't take long for Andrea to figure out they were more than friends. Andrea watched the woman follow in Chet's footsteps as he walked toward the TV remote. *She's no stranger to him!*

"Andrea?" Lila asked.

Andrea forgot Lila was in the room. Had she asked her a question? "Hmm? I didn't hear you."

Lila's eyes widened. "I asked if you knew everyone who came to the party today."

Andrea pulled her attention away from the couple to her friend. Yes, she had recognized many of Chet's friends from the afternoon on the ski hill. People she now considered her friends too. Like Chet explained, even a few of the inn's guests decided to sit in on the game. "Everyone except…" Her eyes returned to Chet and the mystery woman.

Lila must have read her mind. "Oh. That's Olivia Hawkins." The tone in Lila's voice told Andrea what she'd suspected. It spoke volumes.

Andrea ran the name through her memory bank. *It*

rings a bell. Then it hit her. Of course, Chet's old flame.

Lila was quick with an explanation. "A fling. Lots of fireworks between them but nothing more."

"That flame doesn't look quite extinguished." When Chet finally gave his full attention to Olivia, Andrea turned away, not witnessing his response to the attractive woman. Her first impression of Chet was playing out to be true right before her eyes. *I should've known better. I should've listened to my instincts about him.*

Lila gave her a knowing look. "Most men take to Olivia. You can see why. She's hard to resist. I thought he had ended it with her, but you know how those things go."

"Oh, yes, I can see what's going on with my own eyes." Olivia wore a pair of dark spandex jeans paired with a deep-v-cut *Packers* lace-up tee. Both were form-fitting. She stood tall thanks to the knee-high boots that matched the leather belt cinching her tiny waist. Her auburn hair was pulled up into a messy bun with loose tendrils falling to her shoulders. Andrea heard Chet's reason for staying with Olivia ringing in her ears, 'Easy on the eyes," he'd said, or something similar from a male perspective. Now Andrea had no trouble understanding what he'd meant.

"Would you like me to introduce you?" Lila asked.

Andrea shook her head. "No. You go ahead. I wouldn't want you to keep your new husband waiting."

Lila agreed, "He's a keeper, isn't he? Warming up the jeep for me."

Andrea agreed, pleased Lila had found so much happiness in her new marriage. "He certainly is." She caught Chet's nod for her to join him. "This should be interesting. He wants me to come over." She whispered in her friend's ear as she gave her a hug goodnight.

Lila slipped on her coat and headed for the door. "She's no match for you, my friend."

Andrea shook her head, already judge and jury. She might have allowed herself to fall for Chet, but she had every intention of remedying that situation right now. What was she thinking would happen between them? That she and Chet would ride off into the sunset together? "That hardly matters. I have a life that needs tending back home. My career has always been my top priority."

Lila gave her a downturned smile. "Don't be so quick to judge and turn away from a relationship that could be healed with an explanation. I'll see you tomorrow for our meeting."

"I should be there at one o'clock," Andrea said. Lila was probably right. Maybe she should be open to Chet's perception of the situation even though appearances told Andrea everything she needed to know. She turned toward the living room and headed in Chet's direction.

When she approached, Chet offered a hand in Olivia's direction. "Andrea, I'd like you to meet Olivia Hawkins. Olivia, this is Andrea Lockhart, a good friend of Lila's."

Andrea accepted the handshake from Olivia but noticed how quickly she closed the gap between herself and Chet before making the gesture. The message was loud and clear.

Olivia's full lips parted and revealed perfect teeth. "Chet tells me you've been quite a help here at the inn. It was kind of you to stay on and get him out of a difficult situation."

The fact that Chet filled Olivia in on the details of

their arrangement acted as fuel to the smoldering fire inside of Andrea. She had no intention of making the conversation between them easy. "I'm sorry?"

"Helping out until the permanent innkeeper arrived," Olivia's tone implied she'd known the plan's details from the very beginning. "I guess this means you can return home."

Chet must have sensed the awkwardness between them because he cleared his throat trying to reset the conversation. "Olivia was in the middle of a story about one of her cold cases. You've got to hear this," he said, and Andrea sensed he was trying to tighten the slack on this tightrope between them.

I can't stay. Whatever she was feeling was beginning to spin out of control, making it hard for her to breathe. She needed to cut her losses, to save herself. "It's been a long evening, and I'd like to review the binder I made for the new innkeeper."

"Binder?" Chet asked, shifting his weight toward Andrea.

Andrea nodded. "I thought it would be helpful to catalog some of the new processes I developed and helpful hints."

Chet's eyes widened. "I didn't expect you to do that. Thank you."

"How unfortunate you're leaving us," Olivia said, interrupting the discourse. The 'us' Olivia used with purpose reminded Andrea to keep moving, forward and away. She watched Olivia's gaze on the man standing next to her and brushed her fingernail around the nape of his neck. He didn't brush the touch away.

Andrea wanted to do it for him. Instead, she focused on slowing her racing heart. This is what Chet is all about, what he wanted, and it couldn't be clearer. He *was* the ladies' man she pegged him for all along. *How could I have been so blind? So stupid?* Maybe she had let herself slip, but her good sense was flowing back into her brain. All she wanted to do now was get away from him, to run. "I'll say my goodnights then."

Chapter 21

Andrea's cell phone buzzed in her pocket on Monday morning as she made her way to the kitchen. *Jim.* She inhaled a big breath and answered, "Hey, good morning, Jim."

"Morning. I'm the bearer of good news this morning. Are you ready for this? You certainly deserve some after what happened with the merger."

Andrea's pace slowed. She had a pretty good clue of where Jim was going. At least, she hoped so. "Let's hear it."

"I have some bites on a couple of good positions for you. I'll set up interviews if you can get back here by Friday."

"I'll be there," Andrea said with a firmness that must've surprised him.

"Ready to come home then?"

"You bet I am."

Moments later, Andrea walked into the kitchen, dragging an unwanted emptiness with each step. *Why does the thought of going home feel so hollow?* She forced a smile on her face and found the new innkeeper, Dory, dressed in a full-sized apron, ready to get started. She placed the binder of essential duties and procedures she'd created on the kitchen island and got to work.

It wasn't until later in the afternoon on Tuesday that Andrea ran into Chet in the kitchen. On Monday, he'd traveled down to Sturgeon Bay to pick up new reins for the sleigh and spent the night at his brother's. Flashbacks of Olivia and Chet at the party filled her mind, fueling her imagination. She was preparing a sandwich to quiet her growling stomach when she heard footsteps approach from behind. Instincts told her it was him.

"I was afraid I'd missed you and wouldn't get the chance to say goodbye," Chet said.

Chet's words slowed Andrea's hands. Although she intended to leave him a short note and not a formal goodbye, now she had to face him.

"There's not much to say, is there? Dory's training is complete. She has a wonderful sense of humor and has made baking her new hobby. She's a perfect fit. But, I do want to thank you for the opportunity to have learned an entirely new trade," she said, trying to lighten the moment.

His steps drew closer. "You never know when you might need it." His voice was already causing an ache deep inside of her. *How long will I miss hearing his voice?* She fought the urge to turn and face him. Instead, she placed the top back on the mayonnaise jar.

"I came by this morning, but you looked busy with Dory. I stopped again in the afternoon but found you'd left for a meeting. You're a hard woman to track down."

Andrea strengthened her resolve. She could ask for an explanation for the scene she'd witnessed on Sunday between Chet and Olivia, but what would be the point? He should live the life he was meant to live, even if his choices meant it didn't include her.

"How does a sleigh ride sound before you leave? I

need to break in the new reins I picked up yesterday and convince Dad that this was a good investment. Maybe if he saw it for himself, it would make my task easier."

Last night's new-fallen snow blanketed the property with four inches of fresh powder. The air would be crisp and clean, and Andrea could already feel the exhilaration of a ride. But, as tempting as it was, she couldn't. Instead, Andrea gazed out the kitchen window, hoping to strengthen her resolve. She cared for Chet more than she wanted to admit, but Andrea couldn't allow him to sway her from the truth any longer. She'd been wrong about him – terribly wrong, and he'd shown that to her the night of the party. Besides, it was time she returned to the reality of *her* life.

He inched closer. "It'll be a beautiful night, clear, with lots of stars, and I picked up one of those thick blankets on my way home so you wouldn't get cold." His voice was so velvety, so smooth.

Andrea heard the persuasion. She fought the automatic response to make things right between them. *It doesn't matter anymore.* With her focus back on her career, she had no intention of being swayed by Chet's smooth talking. He was good at this game of his, but she was on to him now. "I don't think that's a good idea. I have a meeting with Lila tomorrow, and I need to prepare for the interviews Jim is lining up for me on Friday. It's important I get back on point with my life and career. I have the first flight out on Thursday."

She heard his sigh.

"I was hoping to change your mind about that."

She tried to ignore the icicle-thick disappointment she heard in his voice. Instead, she forced the air from the bread bag, twirling it with a tornado-like velocity.

"I'm afraid not. I have a real chance at landing something right away if I act now, but I need to prepare."

He paused. "I see, and everything that happened here between us is out the window?"

Reluctantly, she turned to face him. "Us? There is no *us*. That became very clear Sunday night when your old girlfriend showed up."

Chet raised his hands. "Let me explain what you *think* happened."

Andrea raised her hands to stop him. "I don't need, nor do I want, an explanation. I understand what happened. Besides, it doesn't matter. I'm going home. Back to my life and career, and you should do the same. We had some fun together, but we both know it's over."

"Oh, so we're back to where we started? If you weren't so darn stubborn I...."

She delivered a resounding slap to the side of his face. Was it because of his comment or the hurt she promised herself she'd never feel again?

Chet winced and backed away from her. Without another word, he grabbed his coat and walked out. The door slammed behind him, and Andrea was certain she'd just lost what could have been the love of her life.

Chapter 22

Dragging with her a heavy heart over last night's argument with Chet, Andrea stepped into The Perfect Cup café on Wednesday and spotted Lila seated at a corner table. It provided a full view of Bay Street and the shoppers picking up after Christmas sales. Giant snowflakes fell from the sky, creating a picture-perfect scene. *I'm going to miss this.*

Lila tossed her phone in her purse when she approached. Her eyes lit up when she saw Andrea. It was hard not to notice the look of disappointment that soon followed.

From the corner of her eye, Andrea spotted Cassie. She held various muffins on a large tray and enjoyed conversations with her guests seated at the other tables. Andrea smiled. The café was almost at capacity proving the grand opening had been a success.

"I'm not sure I'll let you go," Lila teased. "It's been wonderful having you in our corner of the world."

Andrea sighed, "I'll miss this place and all the people. You were right about how special it is here. It's like living in a snow globe."

Lila's face lit up. "Wait until you see it in the summer," she suggested as if that were part of Andrea's future.

Over the last couple of days, Andrea had moved into a reminiscent mood, doing her best to remember all the unique nuances of Sister Bay. She adored the wide sidewalks, the friendly faces of local merchants, the steady movement of the waters on the Bay, and the first time she saw the sign that read *Welcome to Taylor Farms B&B*. Despite how things ended with Chet, she'd store these memories in a safe place in her heart.

Lila's eyebrows tweaked upward. "Would you consider coming back so we can hold our meetings in person?"

Andrea placed her coat on the back of the chair. "You know as well as I that you'll be assigned a new agent soon after the holiday break."

"I'm still calling you to run past my crazy storyline ideas, agent or no agent."

Andrea smiled, warmed by the idea. "I'm counting on it. I do have some good news. Jim has lined up a day of interviews for me starting on Friday."

"Terrific," Lila said, but Andrea heard the lack of enthusiasm in her voice.

Cassie approached, "Good morning, Andrea." She filled her cup with steaming coffee from a second carafe on her tray.

Andrea inhaled the familiar scent as she pulled out her chair and took a seat. "Is that…?"

Cassie's smile broadened. "Your favorite roast, Dark Chocolate Cherry. It's becoming my business to remember what my customers enjoy the most."

"Good job," Andrea smiled and was touched to be included in one of Cassie's special groups of people.

"Lila tells me you're going home tomorrow," Cassie

said. She balanced the serving tray on the corner of their table. "Is there anything I can say to change your mind? We need you here!"

Andrea shook her head. "I was just telling Lila that Jim has lined up a day of interviews for me. But, of course, there are no guarantees."

"Excellent," Cassie beamed. "Now, you can take me up on my idea and open up that bookstore you always wanted next door."

Andrea giggled while Lila asked, "What bookstore?"

Cassie bent toward Lila, lowering her voice. "Andrea's had a childhood dream of owning a bookstore."

Andrea raised her hands to stop Cassie from going any further. "It's sweet that you remembered, but I need to go home for more than just that reason." Andrea inwardly frowned. She'd not only miss her best friend but all the new friends she'd met along the way, Cassie being one of them. Watching The Perfect Cup grow into a thriving business, and lending a hand when needed, would have been a pleasure.

Cassie waggled a finger, "If things don't work out, you can always come back here. By the way, I followed up on your lavender idea."

Andrea's ears perked. "You contacted the lavender farm?"

Cassie refilled Lila's cup with a dark roast. "I did, and they're interested. They told me once their visitors disembark, the first request they have is for a hot cup of coffee. Is this perfect, or what? There's a good chance my blends will be their only offerings in exchange for displaying their products here in the café."

Andrea beamed. "It took your initiative to make that happen."

"But it took your idea for me to make a move in the right direction. We'd make a good team," she insisted.

Cassie was right. Andrea had enjoyed brainstorming marketing ideas for her. "If today's any indication, you're off to a good start," Lila added. "You've got a packed house here."

Cassie's eyes widened. "And I'm grateful for it. Speaking of the café, would you ladies like to try one of our muffins? We have our top seller, the Door County cherry or Wisconsin cranberry orange."

The marketing wheels turned Andrea's head clicked into gear. "Where did you get the cranberries?"

"Right here in the county," Cassie replied, then flashed Andrea a curious look. "Wait a minute. I bet I know where you're going with this. Another partnership?"

Andrea reached for one of the sweet cranberry muffins from Cassie's tray. "Sounds like we're on the same track."

"You're going to suggest I contact the vendor and strike up a cross-marketing deal."

Andrea peeled the delicate paper from the muffin. "That's right. I think it's wise to keep looking for opportunities to help your business grow. It's very similar to marketing Lila's books. Bookstores are a given, but other shops and vendor opportunities turn into very lucrative outlets."

"This is what I'm going to miss when you're gone. The idea-making machine in your head!"

Lila followed Andrea's lead, choosing a cherry muffin for herself. "And I don't mind sharing that bright mind of hers. She's been the captain of my little ship of books for years."

"I'll look into the cranberry venture as soon as I get a free minute," Cassie said. "Enjoy your breakfast."

Andrea laid out the last pieces to the marketing plan and book tours for the rest of the afternoon while Lila shared her plot points for the series. It wasn't until Andrea stretched out her shoulders that she noticed they were the last customers in the café. At some point, Cassie must have turned the *We're Open* sign to *Sorry We're Closed*.

"Do you realize we're the last ones here?" Andrea asked.

Lila nodded. "No wonder we held these meetings in our apartments. We don't know when to stop."

"We've covered it all. Not one issue is left open. You can breathe easy and begin writing the first book in the trilogy."

"I can understand why Chet said he'd miss you when you leave."

Andrea stopped the smallest of protests of speaking Chet's name from slipping through her lips. Lila, Conrad, and Chet were good friends. "I have a feeling Chet Taylor will be just fine."

"Conrad believes it was more than your contributions to the inn that he'll miss," Lila added.

Andrea didn't want to open that door. "The inn is in good hands with Dory. I'll admit, in the end, I'm glad I stayed. We managed to cover a lot of ground in the last few days, from your story's outline to a list of sound publishers. I'll be sure to pass it on to the next agent," she said, doing her best to turn the attention away from Chet and back to the meeting.

"So am I. We always did work well together, but I wish you could stay a little longer. We may have some big news to share," Lila said under her breath.

Andrea placed a stack of manila folders back in her briefcase and then turned toward her friend. "You're going to have to tell me now because I have a ticketed flight for tomorrow morning that I have no intention of canceling."

Lila leaned across the small table. "Conrad and I are hoping we made a baby over our honeymoon. We certainly tried hard enough." Lila's eyes twinkled under the lights of the café with her secret.

Andrea's hands slowed with Lila's news remembering Chet's prediction. Children. If Andrea stayed the course, she would never experience this momentous time of a woman's life, never feel the exhilaration of bringing news of a baby into the world. The closest she would get to this miracle would be as an observer from a distance. Andrea crossed one leg over the other, ignoring the temptation to second-guess her decision to leave. "Lila, that would be fantastic," she said, filled with both joy for her dear friend and regret for herself at the same time.

Lila nodded. "You're the first person I told. We decided to get started on a family right away, especially if we want more than one, which is the case."

Chet was right! "That makes perfect sense." Andrea agreed as she followed Lila's lead, slipping on her coat and gloves.

"Call me and let me know how the interviews go. I want a promise that you'll come back soon."

Andrea inwardly sighed. With a new agent soon assigned to Lila and Chet back with Olivia, coming back to the little village in Wisconsin looked unlikely for Andrea. "I will, and I'll try. But, first, I need to focus on knocking the socks off the interview committees and land a new job," Andrea said, surprising herself for using one of Chet's lines when they first met.

Gazing outside, Lila said through a breath, "I guess it's that time, isn't it?" She slipped her knit hat on her head.

"Your new husband will want his supper," Andrea teased. She hugged her friend for the last time and realized she'd be leaving a big part of her heart in this little village in Door County.

Chapter 23

Andrea's flight lifted off the ground at six a.m. early Thursday morning. She rubbed at her tired eyes, feeling the effects of an early start to the day. When they reached a cruising altitude, she pressed the *Recline* button, thankful for the light blanket she accepted from the flight attendant. She draped it over her body and allowed her eyelids to close.

Dreamlike images floated mistily through her mind. Lila came into view waving goodbye after their meeting yesterday at the café. Cassie stood behind her, smiling. Then she shook Michael's hand on her first visit to the inn. She raced down the toboggan hill, clinging to Chet all over again. His broad shoulders and muscular arms were steering their path. His laughter joined with hers. She heard Conrad's sound advice ringing loud and clear. The playfulness of cardinals in the evergreen trees filled her view and the peaceful tranquility that filled her. It wasn't until Chet's face came into focus that her eyes fluttered open. If only she hadn't reacted as she had with him the last she saw him. Regret filled her. *Now, it's too late.*

"Ladies and gentlemen, we are beginning our descent into LaGuardia Airport, where temperatures are…." The pilot's announcement gave Andrea a start. She watched the rising sun stream through the small window onto her face.

I'm back.

~

She's gone. Chet turned the steering wheel of his truck a little too sharp and tore into the parking lot of The Perfect Cup, fully aware he was traveling too fast. He slammed on the brakes and slid to a stop, almost sideswiping the *Handicapped Parking* sign. After walking into the café, he heard Conrad teasing his sister, Cassie. The lonesome feeling he'd been carrying around in the pit of his stomach lifted. "Hey, man, why don't you pick on someone your own size for a change?"

"Oh, you mean you? Bring it on," Conrad jeered. "What are you doing here?"

Chet surveyed the room. He'd hoped to grab a seat at the counter, but now that looked unlikely. Although he enjoyed talking with Conrad, the foul mood following him around had him hoping Conrad was on his way out. Chet turned in his direction to answer his question. "I'm heading over to Lambert's. I need a couple of clevis fasteners for the sleigh. Thought I'd grab a cup of coffee first."

"And I stopped in for a free cup off my sister. She promised me if I finished the remodeling of the place, I'd have a bottomless cup of coffee coming for the rest of my life. Isn't that right, Sis?"

Cassie steered her gaze from her brother in Chet's direction. "That's right, and he hasn't wasted any time collecting. Morning, Chet, the regular?"

"Sounds good," Chet agreed.

Cassie pushed a pencil behind her ear. "Why don't

you two take the table over by the window, and I'll bring your coffees right away."

So much for solitude.

"The regular? What am I missing here?" Conrad asked. He pulled a chair and seated himself at the table. "You coming down *here* for breakfast now?"

Chet removed his coat. "Yeah, I thought I'd switch it up for a while and help Cassie out." Of course, that wasn't the whole truth, but he'd managed to convince himself otherwise. The truth was, breakfast wasn't the same without Andrea. He'd grown used to seeing her flipping pancakes and sizzling bacon first thing in the morning. Then she always made a point to sit down and chat with their guests. She said they'd appreciated the time she took to spend with them. She was right. It was one of the most favorable and frequent comments in their reviews. With the new system she implemented, they could track their peak seasons and adjust the rates accordingly. The inn went from a thrown-together operation to running like one of his fine-tuned machines in the shop, but somehow even that managed to fall flat for Chet without Andrea by his side.

Conrad threw him a questionable look. "Nice of you," he said.

Chet steered his focus back to his friend and off his troubles. He drew from his well-oiled sense of humor. "I'm told I'm a nice guy."

"Is that right?" Conrad gave him a smirk. "How's single life treating you?" Conrad's eyes bore into Chet's.

"Staying single, that's the plan."

As more guests piled into the little restaurant, Cassie approached, carrying a tray. She poured coffee and then slid a plate in front of Chet.

Chet narrowed his gaze on the quick bread. "That doesn't look like cherry," he said, recognizing the sound of a complaint in his voice.

Cassie rested a hand on her hip. "We're fresh out of cherry. We have banana nut and cranberry orange today. I figured you for a cranberry man." If the smile she gave him could've been a tool of persuasion, she'd won the argument.

Chet nodded, disappointed in how he responded to his friend's sister. How long would it take for him to snap out of this? He had to try at least and make an effort. Maybe that would be enough to get his life back. "Good guess. Thanks."

"Don't thank me. It was all Andrea's idea. First, she encouraged me to contact the lavender farm and propose a cross-marketing partnership. And it worked. As soon as she spotted the cranberries in the muffins, she suggested the same arrangement. Because of her, I have two new businesses selling my coffee blends."

All that didn't surprise Chet. "Seems she was a big help to you, too."

Cassie placed a small basket of extra muffins in the center of the table. "She was. I miss her already. I tried talking her into opening up a bookstore in the building next door now that she's looking for a new job."

Chet's ears perked up. Then he remembered Andrea telling him about the bookstore she'd wanted since she was young.

Cassie rambled on. "She was set on interviewing back home for a new position. I was hoping she'd fall for you, Chet, and we could keep her around," Cassie threw him a half-smile.

Me too. "I think she has other priorities."

Cassie took a step backward. The surprised look on her face was hard to miss. "That's too bad. You're not losing your touch, are you?" she teased.

Chet huffed and swallowed his first sip of the coffee Cassie had poured him. Even the smooth breakfast blend left a bitter taste on his tongue. The bad mood he was trying to ditch rose, welcoming him back. *What next?*

Cassie's eyes scanned the room. "I'll check with you in a bit. Got to run."

Conrad drained his coffee and then refilled his cup from the carafe on the table. "You can't blame Andrea for bolting. You didn't give her much choice."

The last of Chet's resolve snapped. He didn't want to hash over the details of how it all went down with Andrea, but Conrad was way off here. "*I* didn't give her much of a choice? What's that supposed to mean? You heard what Cassie said. She was determined to get back to start interviewing for a new job."

Conrad threw him a skeptical glance. "That's not the whole truth, and you know it."

Chet wasn't about to let Conrad's attitude slide. If he had something to say, he should damn well say it. "What are you getting at?"

"It didn't help you hooking up with Olivia again," Conrad said under his breath.

"What?" Chet gave the room a once over and found it was packed. He leaned in and kept his tone low. "Where'd you hear that?"

Conrad gave him a serious look. "Lila mentioned that she and Andrea practically had a front-row seat to the show."

Chet's back hit the chair. He returned a blank stare at his friend. He reframed past events to figure out what *show* Conrad was talking about. "When did that supposedly happen?"

Conrad took a monstrous bite from his muffin, then washed it down with his second cup of coffee. "The night of the playoff game. I went out to warm up the truck. Lila said Andrea was as angry as she'd ever seen her. She refused to talk to Lila about it again. It was back to the job from that point on. Your name was off-limits."

The playoff game. Chet cursed under his breath as the pieces of the night came together. Andrea must've seen Olivia trying to work her way into his arms again.

"That's not what happened?" Conrad asked. "I mean, it wouldn't surprise me if you ended up back with Olivia."

"No, that's not what happened. At all. But it doesn't matter now. Andrea's gone."

Conrad's eyes widened. "You let her go?"

"Her mind was made up, and it didn't end well." Chet rubbed a thumb down his jawline, remembering the slap. "But her anger makes sense now. She misread what happened between Olivia and me, and then she must've assumed the worst."

Conrad's face broke out in a grin. "Jake told me about the afternoon on the ski hill. From what I heard, you two hit it off. Said she stuck with you like a second skin."

"Geez, Jake doesn't know when to keep his mouth shut. Her tobogganing skills were rusty. So, of course, we partnered up."

"And the wipeout?" Conrad asked. He didn't even try to hide the widening smile spreading across his face.

Chet knew Conrad well enough that the man would wait for his answer as long as it took. Despite Jake interrupting them, how many times had he wished he'd flat-out kissed her that day? The tender, vulnerable look in her eyes told him they'd moved beyond all the roadblocks and had fallen for each other. If not for Jake and his untimely arrival, maybe he wouldn't be in the position he found himself in now, and everything would be different.

An old country favorite blared from the jukebox filling the café along with hoots from nearby customers. He wished he could go back in time and change the course of events. Remembering the wipeout, Chet couldn't stop an answering grin.

Conrad nodded. "I thought so. Listen, I'm going to give you some advice you can take or leave. Don't make the same mistake I did and not go after the woman you've fallen in love with. I could've saved myself and Lila years of grief if I had followed my heart and not my stubborn bullheadedness. I paid for that mistake dearly. God's trying to lead here, so all this works out for His good. It's no accident that Andrea ended up here in Sister Bay or stayed on as long as she did, just like it wasn't a coincidence that Lila came back to help out Melanie."

Chet shook his head. Ever since his return home, he'd committed to becoming a better man, an honorable man. "When you compete with a career, you walk down a lonely road. It may work for some, but not me."

"Maybe her career is the easier of two roads for her. The question is why she left when she did. You can't let that go. She needs to know the truth. You owe her that much."

Chet's resistance slowed. Conrad may have a point. For the first time, he considered the impossible. He ran a hand across the back of his neck, attempting to ease the paralyzing tension building since Andrea left. "Even if I wanted to go after her, I wouldn't know where to look. It's not like she left me her address."

Conrad chuckled as if Chet had told him a good joke. He reached for a second muffin. "That, my friend, is the easy part."

Chapter 24

Later that afternoon, Chet let out a curse at the same time his dad opened the door and walked into the shop.

Michael stomped off the snow on his boots. "You want to get it off your chest?" His father closed the door behind him and walked toward his son.

"There's nothing to talk about," Chet said and tossed the pliers onto the workbench. It rattled to a stop against an oil can. Since the conversation with Conrad, he couldn't keep his mind focused on the simplest tasks. *Pathetic.*

His dad handed him a plate of scrambled eggs, bacon, and a side of toast. "Go ahead and eat. Food has a way of settling a man's nerves."

Chet removed his gloves. *He's always here when I need him, even when I don't ask.* "Thanks, Dad."

Michael strode in the direction of his son's work project. The cobalt blue sleigh gleamed under the shop's fluorescent lighting. "Seems to me that your mood is as foul as a bucket of fish gone bad ever since Andrea left."

Chet bit into the buttered toast. The last conversation he wanted to have was about Andrea. "I didn't sleep right last night, that's all, and now it looks like I need new clevis fasteners for the reins to fit snug, which means another trip to town."

"Uh-huh." Michael gave Chet a long look before running his hand along the side of the sleigh while Chet finished his food. "You've done a fine job with the repairs on this old rig, and after the polish, it'll almost look brand-new."

"You didn't think it was a good idea when I brought it home. What changed?" Chet placed his empty plate on the workbench and swallowed the rest of the toast with cold coffee. Even he didn't like the argumentative tone in his voice. *What am I trying to provoke here?*

Michael turned his head and gave Chet a serious look. "There was a time I knew what was best for the farm and its future, but that time has come and gone."

Chet stuffed his hands in his pockets and gave his dad his full attention. Whatever was on his mind must be important, or he wouldn't have come down here. Ever since his stroke, he preferred staying in the office, where it was comfortable and warm.

"I've been giving an idea of mine a whole lot of thought. Talked to your mother about it again last night. Course, she's thrilled."

Chet shook his head. He wasn't following. "Dad, what's this all about?"

"It's time you took over. You need to start living your dreams for the farm. The same way I did when I bought the place. You've got more to handle now with the inn and that pole barn idea you've got cooking in your head. But I can see how your ideas will bring in money that'll save us." Michael waved in the direction of the outbuilding. "I can't keep up with it all." His dad blew out a tired breath.

Chet paused, letting his father's words sink in. "I had no idea you were thrashing all this through. Why didn't you talk to me early on?"

"Timing. It was all about timing. Andrea helped you believe in yourself, and a fire began burning inside of you again. All your dreams for the place became crystal clear with her help. That's what I was waiting for before turning things over to you. That clarity and vision to come back that you used to have for the place. Your brother never wanted to be a part of the farm, and we accepted that. But it's in your blood, Chet. It always has been and always will be."

Chet swallowed the lump in his throat while searching for the right words. He remembered his foolhardy plan to make it rich in Vegas playing cards. He'd lost it all, every last dime. "I was so blind, Dad. Out of my head, thinking I could be something I'm not, instead of grabbing hold of who I was. When Chuck showed up in Vegas and told me you needed me at home, I couldn't believe it. When I'd run myself out dry, you still wanted me back."

Michael threw up his hands. "That was no coincidence either. All those mistakes you think you made years ago taught you how much the place means to you. God uses everything for His good. It wasn't your brother who dragged you back home. God taught you a powerful lesson then, just like He's trying to do now."

Chet wasn't sure he followed. "I was with you on the mistakes part, but now you lost me. What is God trying to tell me?"

His dad strode toward him. His chest puffed up under his flannel shirt. His cheeks went fire-red. "Your *girl*, Chet. Andrea! You let the best thing that ever happened to you walk right out of the place."

"She's not my girl," Chet argued. "You know she's committed to her career."

Michael's hand landed hard on the workbench, almost tipping over the oil can. "Diddly squat. That doesn't mean anything. Do you get my meaning? She's not married to her work, and you know that."

Chet's confusion rolled into disbelief. His dad couldn't be suggesting what he was thinking. "You expect me to go running after her?" Chet asked certain his dad would suggest otherwise.

"Damn right I do," Michael barked right back. His eyes locked in on his son's. She's not like Olivia, and you know it when you're honest with yourself. Not how she took to the place and fit right in as innkeeper, helped Cassie out at the café, and had the time of her life putting the tailgate together with us. And that's just what I know. Add everything you know, and you've got yourself the right girl."

Chet's mouth dropped open. Then, hooking the leg of a nearby stool, he drew it close and sank into the seat. He didn't want to miss what was coming next.

"Why should you be any different than the rest of us?" Michael shook his head to accentuate his point. "You already know the story of your mother and me and how I had to beg for her hand. I had to prove I was worthy of being her husband. If that's not enough, look what Conrad went through. Haven't you learned a thing? You've got to fight for what you want."

His dad's argument sounded all too familiar. *Isn't that what Conrad had told him earlier?* Chet stared at his boots, trying to make sense of his dad's advice. "Even if I considered doing such a fool thing, I can't be running off to New York now. The trucks are ready with deliveries. Our schedule couldn't get any tighter."

"Your brother's already on his way. Said he was planning on coming up here anyway to see your mother now that she's home from Arizona."

Chuck wants to see their mom made sense but working the orders? It had been a long time since he worked on the farm, too long.

His dad must have read his mind. "I'll help him out. No need for you to worry. Consider it my last official duty as president and CEO of the place before my retirement. After that, you're in charge."

Chet couldn't stop popping up off the stool, closing the distance between him and his dad. He wrapped his arms around him like a kid and gave him the bear hug of his life.

"Don't kill me before I get the chance to call it quits, or your mother will have your head!" Michael yelped, feigning defeat.

Chet released his hold. "And she would!" His laughter mixed with his father's, sounding like an old familiar song to Chet's ears. His dad believed in him again. The slate was now clean. When the moment lightened, Chet realized this was what he'd been waiting for, praying for—his father's forgiveness. "I'll make you proud, Dad."

Chet saw his father's lips go taut, holding back raw emotions.

Michael shook his head. "Already am. Now listen, when you find yourself in a bind with this business, and you will, remember what I told you." He raised a thumb upward. "Shoot off a prayer and wait for His answer. You do that, and you'll be okay."

Chet didn't need words to respond to his dad's good advice because he was already practicing the fruitful habit. He'd taught him so many things, and now that time was over. It was Chet's time to step up and take the lead.

Michael zipped up his parka.

Before heading for the door, he placed a hand on Chet's shoulder and squeezed. "Now go get your girl, Son."

Chapter 25

Andrea picked up her pace as she walked down the jet bridge leading to the terminal. The third week in January, usually cold and crisp and bright from reflective snow, would be moving into a thaw over the next week. After that, temperatures would soar into the mid-40s. She hoped the forecast would brighten her outlook, as it had in Door County.

The first person to come into view was Jim. "How was your flight, kiddo?" Jim asked.

Andrea's heart softened at the cute nickname Jim had given her years ago. "Uneventful, which gave me time to prepare for tomorrow's interviews." As they walked, the memories of the little village of Sister Bay and the people who lived there began to fade. The sense of loss she'd been struggling with the entire flight began to loosen its grip on her heart. *I'm back where I belong.*

Jim's long legs stretched out in front of him as they moved toward the baggage carousel at a quick clip. Andrea hustled to keep pace, regretting the heels on her feet, and missing Chet's hand on the small of her back to guide her. "So, what's the schedule for tomorrow?" she asked.

Jim stopped in the middle of the walkway and faced

her, forcing other travelers to step around them. "You have two interviews in the morning and one in the afternoon. Monday's panning out too. I just need to follow up on a few calls now that you're back home."

Andrea scanned the soaring ceilings in the terminal dotted with brand-new LED lights. The cool palette of grey tones was in severe contrast to the green tin roofs and apple-red barns she'd grown used to in Door County. *So colorless.* They walked past a sentry of artificial plants landscaping the hallway, creating a crisscross pattern of sunlight streaming through tinted windows. *No cardinals in those trees.* At least the warmth of the sun felt good on her face.

"If you land one of these positions, you'll be back on your feet without a blink."

Jim's counsel should have felt better. With his help, this block of interviews could turn things around for her, but Chet's smile on the face of another passenger distracted her. A pull so strong to another life, in another place, with another man, began to overpower her thoughts. How much longer would she be able to deny her heart's content?

Andrea gazed outside, doing her best to refocus. While Jim brought her up to speed, Andrea wondered how Dory was coping with a full house of reservations at the inn. *Did I remember to take out the blueberries from the freezer?* She considered a quick text to the new innkeeper reminding her of the hidden case buried behind the strawberries but decided against it.

After retrieving her luggage, Jim hailed a cab. They agreed to meet tomorrow after the interviews and touch base. If they needed a step two, they'd tackle that together. And there was still the remaining accounting left to finish.

When she looked around her flat an hour later, it was as if with new eyes. Like the terminal and the city around her, it reflected the muted winter tones of grey and white in its expansive walls and ceilings. Even the décor she was so pleased with before leaving lacked color.

"I'm home," she called out, but of course, no one answered. There would be no smiling Chet bursting through the door, shaking off the new-fallen snow onto the floor, despite her threats of no breakfast. Mike wouldn't be sitting on a stool, smiling, enjoying their banter. Guests wouldn't be making their way to the dining room for coffee and breakfast. Instead, the apartment seemed enormous, quiet, and empty, just like the life she'd built for herself. How could she have let herself get to this point in life?

After settling in, Andrea lowered her gaze to the glass of wine she'd poured but hadn't touched. When she visited Chet in his shop, the advice he'd often give her was clear, simple, yet accurate. What advice would he give her right now? She wished she could grab a coat and head down to his shop to help her make sense of these conflicting feelings swirling around her, but those opportunities were gone. She'd managed to ruin that with the slap of her hand. She never allowed him to explain, which is what he wanted to do. Shame moved in.

Gazing out her window to the city's lights below, she longed for the same peace and tranquility she'd found peering out the inn's kitchen window. Instead of evergreen boughs laden with snow, she watched a steady stream of lights from the traffic below, a scene that usually invigorated her. She always needed the busyness of the city to feel alive, or so she thought. So why now did it leave her feeling empty and alone, as if the energy source she depended on had gone dry? Despite her short stay in Door County, everything in Andrea's life seemed to have changed. Chet had opened a door she thought she'd sealed shut. The pathway to love and a family she could call her very own.

Andrea turned from the window, guided by an old approach to a new problem. *It's what Chet would suggest I do.* She placed her glass on the coffee table, clicked on the gas fireplace, and took a seat in one of the comfy chairs in the living room. Her heels fell to the floor in a muted thud. Curling her legs under her, Andrea snuggled under the warmth of a warm quilt. Then, for the first time in years, she folded her hands and began to pray.

Chapter 26

Andrea walked into her apartment on Friday exhausted. Her head was spinning. From her point of view, the interviews had gone well, yet she lacked the fever, the motivation, the desire. Her response confused her. *What's wrong with me?*

Last night, she'd closed her eyes and prayed. Surprisingly, those prayers led her back to the end of her first marriage. Why hadn't she worked through the hurt years ago instead of burying her dreams for a family? Deep down, she knew why. It was easy. It helped her avoid all the broken dreams that went along with divorce. But that season of her life was over. She couldn't deny she always wanted a satisfying career, but her eyes were open now to a truth she could no longer deny. She wanted a family too.

She had no idea Chet would open the doors she slammed shut after her divorce. *I get it now.* Andrea welcomed the relief that filled her but was uncertain how Jim would react to what she planned to tell him. She gazed out of the window, wishing to cast her eyes on a cardinal in a large evergreen like she had many times at the inn, but that was nearly impossible. All she saw was traffic. All she heard was the humming of car engines.

Her heart felt as heavy as the dark clouds outside. She kicked off her shoes and headed for the kitchen.

Andrea cracked a few eggs into a bowl while bacon sizzled in the cast iron skillet. After pouring herself a glass of juice, she popped a slice of bread into the toaster. She wished for a jar of raspberry preserves, remembering it was her and Chet's favorite. She smiled with the notion that Door County wasn't so far away and tucked the memory in a safe place.

Thirty minutes later, she arranged her accounting documents on the mahogany table. Throughout her career, she'd worked many tireless hours on this table. Today would be no exception. The lobby phone buzzed. Jim. She was expecting him this afternoon, and he was right on time.

It only took him a few minutes to reach her door. Then she heard the *ring*. He whisked past and strode into the living room, bringing a subtle outdoors scent. He carried his briefcase in one hand and his leather gloves in another. "I want to hear all about the interviews, every detail, don't leave out a thing. How did it go?" he asked. He tucked his gloves in a pocket, shucked snow's sprinkles from his coat, and then handed it to her.

Andrea dug deep for a response that would sound enthusiastic. The fact that she was anything other than overjoyed perplexed her. She turned her attention away from the turmoil inside of her and toward Jim. "I think it went well. I should hear back for second interview appointments sometime early next week."

Jim brought his hands together. "I knew it." It was apparent that Jim was thrilled. She wished she could scoop up some of that enthusiasm for herself. After hanging up his coat, Andrea walked into the kitchen. "It was a day of surprises," she said.

Jim crossed the room, placed his briefcase on the table, and surveyed the documents. "Surprises?"

Andrea placed two glasses of water with a wedge of lemon on the table. "The new owners at Stonewood called and offered me a position."

Jim's eyes went wide. "No kidding?" He took a seat as if the news had caught him off guard. The look on his face told Andrea this was the last thing he expected.

"I suspect it's because the new owners are eager to expand. The job is in Chicago. Arthur's son will run the new site."

"Jack? That little pipsqueak? You've got to be kidding. That's a disaster in the making. He has trouble finding his way back to the office after an off-site meeting, much less lead a brand-new team."

Andrea suspected the same, but she focused on the positives of the offer. "There's a host of other benefits that go along with it – a moving allowance and housing stipend. I think it's clear they want me in Chicago."

Jim huffed. "Of course, they'd have to sweeten the deal for you even to consider it. It's out of the question. We can't work together with that distance, and I promised your father I'd watch over your career."

Andrea knew this was her opportunity. It was right in front of her. "About that. We need to talk."

He must have recognized the seriousness in her voice. He pivoted in his chair to face her.

She took a seat across from him at the table, doing her best to slow her breathing. What she had to say next wouldn't be easy, but there was no turning back now. If she wanted the changes in her life she had to make, it started here. "You've been invaluable to me over the years, and I wouldn't have gotten this far without your guidance and mentoring."

Jim leaned his back into the chair. "Oh-oh. I think I know where this is headed."

Andrea nodded. "We both know it's time I took over the reins of my career. I'm ready."

He gave her a long, drawn-out smile. "Your father told me you'd know when it's time to stand on your own. And you've been ready for a while. Watching you mature in your abilities and make connections on your own has been the fruit of my mentorship with you. This doesn't surprise me."

Andrea felt the tears collecting in the corners of her eyes when she looked at Jim's soft smile. She was so appreciative of all he had done on her behalf. "Oh, Jim, I need one of your famous bear hugs."

He rose with outstretched arms, and with a fatherly tone, he said, "You're going to do all right, kid, wherever life takes you. Keep in touch, won't you?"

Andrea nodded. "You'll know every move I make."

"So, what's next? Have any of the jobs you interviewed for today spiked an interest, or are you leaning toward the Stonewood Chicago post?"

"I want to give it enough time and thought and turn it over in prayer before deciding."

"Prayer?" Jim said in surprise. "I like the sound of that."

Andrea nodded, thinking of Chet. "Someone very special recommended it to me."

Jim's eyebrows waggled. "Is this special person someone you met in Door County?"

Andrea smiled into the eyes of her good friend. "Yes, but I know what you're thinking," Andrea said with a sad heart. "He's not available."

Jim sighed. "Unfortunate. I've been told a man who values prayer is a man to hold onto."

I wish I could. "I know, Jim. I know."

"You up to tackling the accounting work we have left? Give the old guy in the room one last hoorah?"

Andrea smiled. "You bet. Let's do it."

Chapter 27

Chet's flight landed at LaGuardia Airport at 4:15 p.m. on Saturday. He grabbed his duffle from the overhead compartment, sped through the terminal, and caught a taxi. GPS told him the fifteen-mile route to Andrea's apartment on Eighty-Ninth Street could take thirty to sixty minutes, depending on traffic. As they crossed over the East River, Chet began to panic. He hadn't expected rush hour traffic on a Saturday.

A blur of cars and trucks blew past. A vast country road no longer stretched out in front of him; instead, three lanes of traffic followed in domino succession, all heading to Manhattan. The constant dance of impatient cabs, cutting around buses and slower-paced commuters, worked against Chet's peace of mind. It reminded him of the life and the man he'd left behind in Vegas.

Not once had he regretted coming home, but if he were honest, he hadn't orchestrated that return. When his brother, Chuck, showed up, Chet was waiting tables at a steakhouse six nights a week to make ends meet. But he always made sure he had his name in for the next big game to win back his losses. As if he hadn't learned enough over the five years he'd been out there. When Chuck told him their dad *needed* him home, something clicked inside Chet.

During the years of his absence from his family and farm, he'd never been more miserable or exhilarated as he chased the gambling adrenaline rush. He'd managed to dig himself deeper and deeper into a pit of his own making. Too ashamed to go home, he convinced himself he'd deserved where he ended up in life. He'd always thought it took his dad's stroke and his brother throwing him a rope to lead him back to the life he gave away. *But Dad made it clear. It was all part of God's plan for my life. It all worked together for His good.*

"Lots of traffic today," the cabbie said, interrupting Chet's thoughts. Chet had difficulty believing Andrea found this appealing as he took in the skyscrapers and concrete. It wasn't the woman he'd come to know, the one entranced with the simple frolicking of cardinals outside the inn's window. The woman he'd fallen in love with and hoped had fallen in love with him.

Chet leaned in from the cab's back seat and tried to focus on the route. Chet's agitation grew as traffic slowed to allow more cars onto the congested roadway. Time was not in his back pocket right now. His mind flew forward, trying to imagine the scene ahead of him with Andrea. Without knowing the truth, she might refuse to see him. Conrad had told him Andrea deserved to understand what *didn't* happen with Olivia that night. But that wasn't the only thing she had a right to know. He should have been honest with her before she left. It was time. He didn't want to live without her because no one else made him feel like she did. He finally thought he had found his partner, and he wasn't about to blow it now. He wanted to hold her and make all her dreams come true for the rest of her life. All he needed was a chance.

Traffic started moving, and Chet breathed a little easier. They were almost there. Then the worst-case scenario played out before his eyes. Every car, cab, and bus came to a complete stop.

"Now what?" Chet asked. He heard the irritation in his voice. He glanced down at his wristwatch and hoped to find that time had stopped, but it hadn't. *I should be there already!* The trip inched toward forty-five minutes, which did nothing to ease his nerves. Sweat prickled at the back of his neck as he fought an irrational fear of being too late. Ahead flickering red and yellow lights caught his attention.

The cabbie leaned against the steering wheel and squinted through thick lenses. "Most likely an accident. This kind of thing happens all the time. We've got couriers on bikes, buses, cars, and people on foot, and besides that, this is rush hour."

"On Saturday?" Chet had a hard time believing this. Saturdays were catch-up days for him at home, which meant a leisurely pace to the day.

"Every day is rush hour at this time." His comment did little to alleviate the tension building on Chet's shoulders. The old phrase *the city that doesn't sleep* had more truth than legend. Chet heard the hands on an invisible clock ticking in his head. They were at a complete stop. "Do I have any options other than sitting in this traffic?"

The cabbie removed the matchstick pressed between his lips and pointed across the street. "At this point, you could walk there faster. Head north through Central Park. Follow the bridle path up West Avenue. At the first crosswalk, head left, out of the park. That should put you a block away. You look like a pretty fit guy. Should take you ten, fifteen minutes, tops."

"Let's do it." Chet paid the cabbie and grabbed his duffle.

"Good luck to you."

Chet nodded his appreciation to the driver. Luck wasn't all he needed, more like a miracle. As soon as his feet hit the ground, he zig-zagged his way among the vehicles. Finally, Chet entered the park and started the trek to West Avenue. Although his line of work gave him an athleticism he could count on, he was in unfamiliar territory, and the last light of the day was fading fast. Chet quickened his pace, hoping to find Andrea at home. If not, he'd wait as long as it took. He kept track of his progress in a steady jog and by watching the street signs.

Chapter 28

After pouring herself a cup of hot tea, Andrea headed for the living room. She smiled, remembering Cassie's insistence on bringing the tea sample back home. She lifted the cup to her lips and savored the first sip. Mmm, a hint of honey in the brew. She'd miss watching Cassie's café blossom into a vibrant business in Sister Bay. Just one more item to add to this list, Andrea thought. She took a seat in one of her favorite chairs near the fireplace and placed a call to Lila. *It's late Saturday afternoon, Lila should be home.*

Lila picked up on the second ring.

"Do you have a few minutes? I have news on two fronts, and I want to hear how you're writing is going." Andrea said.

"My writing is on track. I'm about to dive into the sagging middle of the first book in the series, so it's going well. I'd much rather hear about your news. By the way, everyone misses you terribly. If I have to listen to Cassie bemoan your absence one more day," Lila complained, but Andrea heard the humor in her voice.

Andrea wondered if 'everyone' included Chet. Then as quickly as the question popped into her head, she remembered the truth. Chet's lost to her. She mentally switched gears. "Cassie has so much to think about right now, but she'll be fine."

"True. Did she tell you her latest partnership is a tea vendor in Fish Creek?"

"No kidding. I'm enjoying a cup of honey chamomile right now. It's wonderful."

"I've been waiting for your call so we could catch up," Lila said, steering their conversation back to Andrea's news.

Andrea placed her cup on the small table next to the chair, tucked her legs beneath her, and snuggled in for a long chat with her best friend. "What would you like to hear first – the professional or personal?" She clicked on the gas fireplace and heard the *swoosh* of the flame.

"Let's start with the professional. Knowing you as I do, I can imagine that you're not working is weighing against you."

Andrea took comfort in knowing her friend understood her as she did. "I had my interviews yesterday and a job offer from Stonewood."

"I thought Stonewood let you go?"

"They did, and now they want me back. Crazy, right? They offered me a job in Chicago or New York."

Andrea heard Lila's surprise in her gasp. "Chicago? They have an office there?"

"They leased a building and apparently, Jack is going to run the operation."

"Wow. That is a surprise. You don't sound very enthusiastic about all of this. What's going on?"

It felt so good to be an open book with her friend. Finally, the days of hiding the truth and burying her dreams were over. "I'm not sure. Ever since I came home, things feel, well, different."

"Different? How?" Lila asked.

"Something's missing and I'm not sure how to fix things."

"Well, if New York doesn't feel like home anymore, everyone here in Sister Bay wants you back," Lila urged.

Andrea sighed. If only it were that easy. "Well, I'm expecting a couple of second interviews next week, and now I have this job offer with Stonewood to mull over the next few days. I have a lot to think about."

"True, but you've experienced a whole different life here. I went through the same thing."

"But it's not the same. You had Conrad."

"You're right, but I'd love to have you closer. Maybe you should consider the Chicago post. It's only a morning's drive from Sister Bay."

Andrea nodded to herself but wondered how often she'd make the trip. She'd love to be closer to Lila and Conrad, and Cassie, but the village was so small, and running into Olivia and Chet would be something she'd rather avoid. "That's true. I've got some real soul searching to do. I'm going to take a long walk in the park after our call. I found out how much that clears my mind and helps me see things more clearly."

Lila's voice lifted. "Are you referring to all the walks I heard you and Chet took just about every morning?"

Andrea refused to listen to her heart that wanted to whisk her back to those early morning strolls, her love for the outdoors, and the man walking beside her. "The walks, yes, attributing them to Chet, no."

"I see," Lila paused, "We're still not talking about Chet, hmm?"

"I'd rather not. Now that I have my focus back on

my career."

Lila sighed. "Promise me you won't close all the doors on him quite yet."

What is Lila trying to tell me? Then Andrea was reminded of Conrad's advice, similar to Lila's right now. "All right, Lila, I promise."

"Okay, let's tackle what's next."

Andrea sighed, grateful for the change of subject. "I told Jim that it's time I took charge of my career."

Lila gasped, "I couldn't have guessed that in a million years. You just told me he's at the helm with the interview schedules."

"He is, or I should say, was, after today."

"So, why the change? And why now of all times when you need him the most?"

"I had to. I woke up yesterday morning, and I knew the time was now during this pivotal point in my life. Jim said I'd been ready for a long time. It was hard, Lila. He's been my confidante for so long."

"That doesn't have to change completely."

Andrea nodded. The decision she'd made still felt old-sweater comfortable. "That's what I told him."

"How does it feel?" Lila asked.

"Liberating. I feel I'm all grown up now and ready for the world. But, I realized something else too." Andrea reflected on the quiet night of prayer and how that night had changed everything for her. "I realized I never really forgave Ben for leaving. I thought if I forgot about all the dreams I had with him, it would be the best way to get over the hurt from our divorce. It doesn't make much sense now, but it did then."

Lila sighed, "If he hadn't joined the overseas program, maybe things would've been different."

Andrea disagreed. Ben didn't have a selfish bone in his body. On the contrary, it was quite the opposite. His caring nature and need to help the underprivileged took precedence in his life, even over their marriage. "I don't think he intended to end *us*. But our demise was the consequence of his decision." Now that she'd returned to prayer, she understood so much more and was in tune with the peace that came with the understanding.

"A lot has happened in just a couple of days. Your whole life is changing."

"Everything came together like a perfect storm. I was so grateful for Jim after my father retired. He guided my career by helping me make the right moves, introduced me to influential people, and encouraged me to attend the proper functions. I can handle it from here, and Jim's ready to scale back and take more time off. I'm ready."

"Oh, Andrea, this takes tremendous courage."

Andrea moaned. "I'm not going to lie. I'll be making decisions that will affect my life in the future. It's exhilarating and frightening all at the same time."

Lila chuckled. "That's life for you."

"When I was in Door County and stepped into the world you live in, all my old dreams came back into view for me."

"So, my asking you to stay was a blessing in disguise, wasn't it?"

"I think so. It's as if a big part of me has been asleep for a very long time."

"All you need, sleeping beauty, is a handsome prince to come along and plant a kiss on those lips."

Andrea sighed. Since the day on the ski hill, the only lips she wanted on hers were Chet's, but she knew that would never happen. Not now. "I'm not sure New York has any princes for that job. For right now, I have to figure out what to do next. Seems life has a way of opening new doors for us, doesn't it?"

"It certainly does," Lila agreed. If someone would've told us a year ago that I'd be married hoping to be pregnant and you'd be considering a job transfer to Chicago, we never would've believed them."

"We were so set in our careers and lives," Andrea agreed. "It's amazing how much life can change in only a few weeks."

"And for our good, Andrea, remember that. Call me and let me know after you've made your decision."

"I will. And you call when you have baby news."

"You'll be one of the first to know right after my husband and Aunt Cathy," Lila promised.

After the call, Andrea walked to the kitchen with a smile, grateful for the sisterly bond she shared with Lila. She placed her cup in the sink and then glanced at the clock. If she wanted to take that walk, she'd have to leave now. One of her favorite times of the day was twilight, and the lights in Central Park would be coming on soon. She'd better get a move on, or she'd miss it.

Chapter 29

Andrea headed to Central Park with a renewed spirit. The call with Lila had gone well, and although she missed having her close by, she had a mountain of a decision to make regarding her future. The walk would help clear her mind, and she hoped to help her come to a decision. Andrea inhaled a deep, cleansing breath and felt a refreshed sense of calm fill her with each step.

Figuring out her next career move wasn't the only thing on Andrea's mind. She had to find a place in her heart to stow away memories of Chet. In her weakest moments, she'd admit how much she missed him. The sound of his voice rang loud and clear in her head. His quick-witted sense of humor and the banter between them all reminded her of that special time in her life. But it was the camaraderie between them she missed the most – the quiet moments of their walks, the coffee talks, working side-by-side in the kitchen, and brainstorming new revenue streams for the inn. Finally, Andrea sighed away the truth – she loved him.

The last rays of sunlight faded as twilight emerged. Between day and night, this special time would always be her favorite. The fresh, crisp air was like the first cup of coffee in the morning. *This walk is what I needed.*

Tucking her scarf snug around her neck, Andrea turned the corner and headed down West Avenue. A horse-drawn carriage was parked at the curb to attract tourists. Tonight was one of those perfect nights when young men proposed and celebrated anniversaries. She looked at the clear night sky, expecting a sprinkling of stars and a full moon.

Andrea paused and then decided to walk toward the carriage as if drawn to it. It was painted the same pretty blue, like Chet's sleigh. The resemblance was remarkable. Andrea's spirits dampened as her hand slid over the smooth surface and soft upholstery. She imagined a couple snuggled under a woolen blanket. Chet's idea to offer sleigh rides would be a sure thing for the inn. Her heart gave a tug. She'd never get the chance to see it – the sleigh gliding across the hills at the farm or hear the laughter and delight coming from the passengers. She would have to imagine that now in her mind.

The driver gave her a smile from his perch on a wooden bench seat. He tipped his top hat in her direction. "Looks like you may be interested in a ride."

"It's tempting," Andrea said, and it was. She was about to refuse but was interrupted by a question from someone nearby.

"It's almost as nice as mine, isn't it?"

The practiced, rhythmic breathing she'd been enjoying a moment ago came to a complete stop. *I know that voice!*

Andrea froze as the carriage pulled away from the curb to pick up a couple signaling for a ride. In the next blink, she was looking into the eyes of the last man she ever expected to see again. *Chet.* He looked irresistible, from his snug-fitting jeans to the sheepskin jacket he wore. Fitted brown leather gloves were on his hands. He dropped a duffle bag to the ground when their eyes met.

Andrea fought not to run to him. Instead of wrapping her arms around his neck and apologizing for the awful slap, she stood as if frozen. If only she could take the first step. She'd cling to him and never let go. There was a time he would have loved that. But now, Andrea wasn't sure, so she stood frozen in place. Without a doubt, she knew she'd fallen in love with this man but feared the precious knowledge came too late.

He stepped closer, giving her hope.

The heat of his body so close to hers lit a match to every nerve ending in her body. Having him so close made it impossible to deny how much she'd missed him. But he'd shown her who he was the night of the party – a man who enjoyed playing the odds hoping not to get caught. She couldn't forget what she witnessed between him and Olivia. He was a player, and he'd made his choice. Luckily, she had a career to return to once again. That truth gave her a surge of courage. She had to be strong, especially now. "You are the absolute last person I ever expected to see again."

Chet's soft Caribbean blue eyes sought hers. "I owe you an apology." His beautiful lips turned downward.

Is that regret on his face? Andrea wasn't sure. Was her heart already softening? There was something she wanted to tell him. "It's me who owes you an apology. I'm sorry for slapping you. My emotions took over, and before I knew it. It was too late."

"I think I understand what happened and why, and I still want to apologize."

With reluctance, she turned away from him and

resumed her walk. It would be easier for him to leave.

He didn't. "Mind some company?" he asked, chipping away another piece of her resolve.

Andrea shrugged, resuming her walk, not fully understanding why he'd traveled so far to make an apology. If he'd reconciled with Olivia, why did he care what happened between them?

He sidled up next to her. Their stride returned to the steady gait they'd fallen into during their morning walks. It felt familiar and slowed Andrea's frenzied steps. Her heart rate followed. *How does he manage to calm me, even though it's over between us?*

"I wish I could have explained what happened the night of the playoff party."

Andrea drew in a cold gust of winter air right along with a good dose of courage. She picked up the pace as if it would help her outrun the words that would soon reach her ears. He'd tell her he took Olivia back. He might even say he was sorry if he'd led her on. She steeled herself and vowed not to cry. Crying was for teenagers who'd fallen in love for the first time and had their hearts broken. "You don't have to explain anything to me."

"I think you might have arrived at the wrong conclusion about Olivia and me."

Olivia and me. He referred to them as a couple. It pressed on Andrea's heart, making it hard for her to breathe. *But did he say 'the wrong conclusion'?* She had to stay focused. "You have a right to live your life and choose with whom you spend your time. And I have my career as I always have." She was doing her best to remain calm and stop the damage to her heart. If only she could walk faster and create some distance between them. *Help me, Lord, to hear the truth. Please help me be strong.*

She felt the pressure of Chet's hand on her arm, preventing her feet from taking another step. Looking up at him, she did her best to hide the truth she knew he'd see in her eyes. She wished they could go back to the easy days at the inn before it all fell apart when it was pure and natural between them.

"Do I also have the right to spend it with the woman I love? The same sassy, spirited woman I'm looking at right now?" He leaned toward her, pressed a finger to still the twitch over her right eye, and then looked deep into her eyes.

Andrea's breath caught.

Chet placed his hands on Andrea's shoulders. "Nothing happened with Olivia that night because nothing could. My heart belongs to you."

Andrea couldn't keep the schoolgirl smile from spreading across her face. Chet had completely turned everything she assumed upside down in his magnificent, excellent, unpredictable way.

She recognized the tenderness in his eyes. It was the same look when he surprised her with the Packers jersey.

"You captured my heart from day one." His smile widened. "You haven't given it back yet, have you?"

No words came from Andrea's lips as she struggled with a good dose of shame. She hadn't given Chet the benefit of the doubt that night. Instead, she made assumptions based on untruths and suspicion and had run back to where it was safe – to her career like she had for so many years. No more, she told herself. "Chet," she murmured, wiping tears from her eyes, "I've missed you so much. Can you forgive me? I'm sorry. I should've trusted you."

"Can I forgive *you*? I need your forgiveness for letting my pride get between us." He brought her fingers to his lips.

Why had she closed herself off to him for so long? So much wasted time.

"All that matters is right now." He opened his arms.

Smiling through her tears, she melted into his embrace. His strong arms wrapped around her, pressing her close. Andrea felt her legs weaken while Chet's muscles tightened, holding her firm. He'd always be there, now and in the future. She'd never known this kind of powerful love until this moment. She clung to him as he lowered his head toward hers. Her heart hammered in her ears. She'd wanted his kiss for so long.

He lifted her chin, and his lips met hers for the first time, causing the world around her to blur. The sounds of nearby traffic faded away. At that moment, she was one with the man she loved, wrapped in the cocoon of his arms.

"You're it for me," he murmured. His rough-shaven cheek rubbed against hers – his whisper in her ear. "I knew the moment I met you I was in trouble. I couldn't stop myself from falling in love with you."

She touched his face. "And I fell in love right along with you, fighting it all the way," she said, bringing his breathtaking smile back to life. *I'll never have to miss another day of seeing that smile on his face.*

He steered them to a nearby park bench. The expression on his face turned serious. "Ever since I've been a boy, I believed that everything happens for a reason, but when I think about losing you." Chet shook his head.

A big piece of Andrea's heart melted. "I want to be wherever you are. I've been hiding behind my career for so long because it was safe. I even buried my dreams for a family behind that big wall. But, it all fell apart after meeting you."

Chet steered his attention to her. "Tell me about it. I want to know everything."

"I told you how Ben fell in love with the idea of helping those less fortunate. It was a perfect fit for him."

"Honorable, but I would've taken you with me," Chet said.

Andrea nodded. "He tried, but at that time, my dad had used his connections to get me my first job in an agency."

Chet remembered the conversation with his dad in the shop. "The timing was off."

"Yes. Besides, I didn't have the luxury of traveling to Africa, especially after everything my dad did to help launch my career."

Chet leaned in. "What happened?"

"Ben discovered a brand-new passion for his life, but our marriage was the price."

He rubbed a thumb across the knuckles of her hand. "You never told me how you managed."

Andrea shrugged. "I buried myself in my work, and I've been there ever since. All my dreams fell asleep, that is until I met you."

Chet's eyes met hers. "Me?"

Andrea nodded. "The door to those early dreams cracked open when I was in Door County. I saw them in Lila's new life with Conrad and my time with you. It wasn't until I came home that I realized I wanted it all back, but I had to forgive Ben in my heart first. That took some deep soul searching and a long night. I thought of you and what you might suggest if you were standing in the room with me."

"I hope I came through, even if I was a figment of your imagination," Chet said with a wide grin.

Andrea brushed the hair from Chet's eyes. "You did, as you always had. I prayed for the first time in years."

"If I remember right, you gave up on prayer. Said it didn't save your marriage despite how hard you tried."

Andrea nodded. "That's right. Do you remember what you told me?"

Chet kissed the top of her nose. "Remind me."

"You said prayer doesn't mean we always get what we want."

Chet nodded, "That's right."

"And even though that's true. We are still living out God's plan for our lives," she added.

Chet lifted Andrea's hand and brought it to his lips. "Let me ask you, Ms. Lockhart, do you think you and I are part of God's plan for our lives?"

Andrea looked into Chet's rugged face and big, beautiful sea-colored eyes. "I'm not an authority on God's intentions, but I'd like to think so, Mr. Taylor. I want the same things in life that you do."

"Are you talking about someone who'll be crazy for you the rest of your life with a houseful of kids?" Chet sat a little straighter on the park bench. The look on his face was genuine and pure and coming from his heart.

It moved Andrea to a place in her heart that had never been touched. The love she felt for this man was overpowering all of her senses. She returned his smile, no longer caring about the smudged make-up under her eyes or the fresh tears slipping down her cheeks. "Yes, exactly that. I want to use my skills somehow, but I'm betting you and I can figure that out."

He inched toward her, closing the tiny gap between them. "You know there are all kinds of careers out in the world. Cassie can't stop talking about all the marketing ideas you gave her, and the inn is buzzing along beautifully because of all the new programs you implemented. You are a multi-talented woman, Andrea. Didn't you tell me you always wanted to own a bookstore?"

Andrea's eyes widened. She couldn't believe Chet remembered that piece of information about her. "I did," she said through a smile.

"Maybe it's time," Chet suggested. "And you'd still be in the world of books."

And away from the grind.

"Maybe it's time we make all your dreams come true," Chet said. "I've got some news of my own that you're not going to believe."

Andrea turned toward the man that held her heart in his hands. Everything was coming together for them. Her heart was racing, and she couldn't stop smiling at this beautiful man in front of her.

"Dad wants to retire. He told me right before I left."

"Does that mean you've finally forgiven yourself?" Andrea gave him a questioning look.

Chet leaned back against the park bench. "You knew?"

Andrea nodded. "It wasn't hard to figure out. You've been blaming yourself for the lessons you needed to learn."

"Sounds like someone's been reading their Bible."

"Uh-huh," Andrea nodded. "Unbelievable that our lives are coming together like this. I feel so lucky."

Chet chuckled. "We both know luck has nothing to do with it," he said, then he rose to his feet.

Andrea let her imagination run in the moonbeam's light and saw an older version of the man she loved. The weathered age on his face from working years in the outdoors. The rounded shoulders from decades of strenuous work. A man with a flurry of children behind him that she couldn't quite make out, despite how hard she tried. *Our children.*

Chet bent down on one knee. "Andrea Lockhart, I believe we have a life waiting for us. Will you do me the honor and marry me?"

Andrea's breath hitched. She would never forget this moment – how they began and how everything else faded away. She marveled at God's unrelenting love for her. Like her dreams for the future, she'd pushed her alone time with Him to the side. Yet, the moment she folded her hands in prayer and called out, she felt Him right beside her, guiding her to the truth.

With no second thoughts but with a renewed belief that whatever happens in life will come together for His good, Andrea slipped her hand in Chet's. "I will marry you, Chet Taylor, because I love you now, and I will love you forever."

The relief in his smile matched the flurry of excitement inside her heart. In the next moment, she was twirling around in his arms. Then, when his lips touched hers, Andrea knew she had found where she'd always belonged, in Chet's arms.

Chet lowered her to the ground and nodded to the city behind them. "You think we could find an engagement ring for you in this jungle?"

"I have a better idea," Andrea said, "why don't we go home and pick one out there together?"

Chet's eyes sparkled. "You read my mind." He laced his fingers with hers and pulled her close, tucking her arm securely under his as he led them through the park and on their way home.

Chapter 30

Andrea stood between Lila and Cassie, surveying what used to be the pole barn at Taylor Farms. She was pleased with what she and Chet had accomplished in the last few months, renovating the building into a festive banquet hall. It would be the first decision Chet had acted on since taking over the reins of the farm from his dad. The newly designed space would accommodate special gatherings like family reunions, wedding receptions, and Christmas celebrations. This evening, Mike's retirement party would be its inaugural event, and Andrea didn't want anything to go wrong.

"What are your first impressions?" Andrea hoped her friends liked what they were seeing.

Cassie swooned. "Wonderful. I didn't see the *before,* but the *after* has a real country farmhouse feel, which is all the rage now." Her gaze moved to the ceiling. "Who had the idea to paint it black?"

Andrea tilted her head and gazed at the illusion of a midnight sky. "Chet did. The color is called nightscape."

Lila bent her head to get a better look. "It feels like I'm looking through a telescope into our galaxy," she added.

"That's probably due to the strip lighting. The

brightness is controlled with dimmer switches."

"Be careful," Lila warned, "you might have found yourself in a whole new occupation. Again!"

Andrea's smile grew wider. She had to admit she loved the direction her life was moving. It was busy, even a bit hectic at times, but she and Chet had found a new rhythm in life that worked for both of them. "Not to worry. I love getting the bookstore ready to open. It's a dream come true for me. Books and authors still surround me. I love it! But I enjoy helping Chet out with some of his projects, this being one of them."

"And I love that your bookstore will be right next to the café," Cassie added. "All the worrying I did about the right business moving in next door was wasted energy. I should've known better. It was all part of God's plan. Everything is coming together."

Andrea nodded, turning toward Lila. "We've already decided to keep the passway door in our building open, so our customers can peruse both stores at their leisure."

Lila's eyes widened. "You go, girl! What an excellent idea."

Andrea nodded. "Your idea for the bookstore's grand opening and the launch of your children's trilogy book tour is perfect."

Lila basked in Andrea's compliment. "We've always been a good team, Andrea. It's time I gave back to help you."

Cassie ran the flat of her hand along the wall. "I wish I would've thought of adding glitter to the wall paint for the café."

Andrea headed toward her new friend. Before her engagement to Chet, she'd felt a special bond with

Cassie. She hoped their friendship would grow even stronger. "The grey paint was a bit drab, so when the paint tech suggested the glitter, we thought why not?"

Lila patted her baby bump. "We've decided to keep the baby's gender a surprise, so we considered grey for the nursery but decided on sage green instead."

"I've always loved that color," Cassie said. "It reminds me of my mother's fern garden."

Andrea lifted her eyebrows. "Look at that man work," she said, allowing a broad smile to spread across her face. In the months that had passed from Chet's proposal, their love had grown deeper than Andrea could ever have imagined. She felt cherished, unique, and completely loved.

Lila and Cassie's heads turned in Chet's direction. The three watched as he stretched a rope tautly across the room, forcing the muscles in his arms and back to strain against the cotton T-shirt.

Andrea read the words laser printed across the banner, *Happy Retirement, Michael.* "Looks perfect, honey," Andrea shouted across the room.

Lila and Cassie both turned toward Andrea. "Honey?" they asked in unison.

Andrea shrugged her shoulders, not even thinking twice about the pet name she'd given Chet shortly after he proposed. "It suits him."

Lila shook her head, "I like it."

"I envy it," Cassie swooned.

Lila patted Cassie's back. "Don't you worry, now that Andrea will be around, she and I will team up and find you a handsome prince, too."

Andrea tore her attention from Chet to Lila. "What do you mean, 'too'? Are you suggesting that Chet and I are a product of your handiwork?"

"I'm not sure I know what you mean," Lila said. But the familiar grin on her face acted like fuel for Andrea's argument.

Andrea thought about the events that led her to Chet. She began to slide the pieces of the puzzle together. As if a light bulb was turned on, she knew what had happened. *Oh my gosh.* "Of course. You deliberately placed us at the same dinner table at your wedding reception, didn't you?"

Lila shook her head, avoiding Andrea's gaze. "That was a coincidence." She smoothed away nonexistent wrinkles from her pretty yellow-and-black polka-dot dress.

She's grinning. Andrea decided to follow her instincts. "And your insistence that I extend my stay because you needed help switching genres?"

"Don't be silly. You've always helped me in the past in the very same way."

Andrea paused. *That much was true.* "Then there's the obvious, of course, your idea that I fill in at Chet's B&B. Another suggestion you insisted on."

"You could have said no," Lila said through her giggles, causing Cassie to join her.

"And argue with the bride on her wedding night? Chet insisted against doing that." Andrea managed to say between her chuckles.

"That's our Lila," Cassie added. "A matchmaker behind the scenes."

"You love me for it all the more, don't you?" Lila asked. "I knew you and Chet were meant for each other."

Andrea grabbed her friend in a hug, "You bet I do. As stubborn as I was, I ended up with my prince."

Cassie sighed. "Apparently, I need all the help I can get."

"If fairy tales can come true for Lila and me, they certainly can for you too," Andrea said reassuringly. With a little help, she and Lila had found their soulmates as far as she was concerned.

Lila nodded. "Andrea's right, but we'd better go find Conrad. People are taking their seats. It looks as if the evening is about to start."

"Talk later," Andrea said as she watched her two friends meander through the crowd. For the first time in a long time, she had found her place. She searched for the man who made that all possible for her and then heard his footsteps. When his arms slipped around her waist and pulled her close, her body recognized his. She laid her head back on his chest.

"Can you believe we'll be standing in this very room celebrating our wedding this fall?" he asked.

"I didn't believe I'd actually be the next to marry when I caught Lila's bouquet."

Chet released a long exhale. "I tried to tell you not to run from tradition. It has a way of tracking you down."

"The only thing that has tracked me down is a handsome organic farmer/B&B owner from Door County."

Chet released a hearty laugh, causing another smile to spread across Andrea's face. She'd never have to miss his laughter again.

After a moment, he asked, "Regrets so far? After all, you walked away from a hard-fought career to opening a bookstore."

His lips found that sensitive spot at the base of her neck, sending a charge through her body. *Is he kidding?*

"Not a one," she said. She could barely remember her life before his love for her and hers for him. Everything had worked out for the best.

"Mmm," he murmured.

"You're spoiling me," she said, enjoying her body's signals.

"I haven't even started yet," Chet whispered.

That sounds like a luxurious promise.

Andrea relaxed in his arms. She visualized toting a baby carrier into the bookstore with a golden retriever on her heels. Then, she turned to him and looked into his ocean blue eyes, "Thank you for loving me, Chet."

Andrea fought to remember where she was when his lips found hers. He had a way of carrying her off to the most beautiful places in her mind.

"Are you two kids going to stop making googly eyes with each other and give me a hand here?" Michael teased. He waited at the base of a small staircase leading to an expansive platform that would act as a stage.

Chet moved toward him.

"Why didn't you build handrails on this thing?" Michael grumbled once his son reached his side.

With strong arms, Andrea watched Chet support his father up the stairs. It was another part of what she admired about the man she'd soon marry. She listened to the engaging banter between father and son.

"They are a pair, aren't they?" Chet's mother gave Andrea a warm smile. They'd had several heart-to-heart conversations since Shirley's return from Arizona. Andrea looked forward to the future and the coffee they'd share at the kitchen table.

"They certainly are," Andrea agreed.

"I have you to thank for this moment." Shirley

waved a hand toward the beautifully decorated room, now full of family, friends, and business acquaintances. Her gaze moved to Michael. "I've been encouraging him to retire for the last five years, but he wouldn't budge until Chet was ready. It took you to make that happen."

Andrea laid a light hand on her chest. "Me?" Andrea shook her head. "I suspect Chet was more than capable of running the farm before I came into his life."

"I'm not talking about his capabilities." Shirley let the moment rest, and her point resonate. Her hazel eyes sought Andrea's. "Chet was a headstrong, determined young man. He always seemed to know what he wanted out of life. The missing piece was the grounding and support from someone who would walk side-by-side with him through life. A partner who believed in him and loved him with a passion. That person is you. After you two met, I heard that truth in Chet's voice in our first phone call."

Andrea's heart softened more for the woman standing next to her. "Your son has given me so much more. He helped me to see the truth about my life. He's drawn me into a thoroughly satisfying love that I can't wait for in the future. I love him with everything that makes me who I am."

Chet's mother beamed. "I hope you have the privilege of this moment one day, knowing you can truly let go because you believe the child you brought into this world will be okay." Andrea squeezed Shirley's hands in hers, appreciative of the highest compliment she'd ever received.

When the lights flickered, the last guests took their seats. Shirley beamed a broad smile. "That's my cue to sit down. He wants me front and center. Will you join me?"

Andrea shrugged. "For whatever reason, Mike asked me to wait here in the wings."

"If I know my husband, I'm sure he has a good reason," she said and moved toward the front of the room with a promise to talk after Mike's address.

Andrea watched Mike walk to center stage to the audience. It didn't show if he was anxious about addressing a crowd this size. Instead, he sat on a wooden stool and, in his easy conversational manner, painted a picture of his early working years in New York in sales and the decision that led him to a farm in Door County. He had no regrets. The audience's smiles and occasional claps showed Andrea they enjoyed his message. Mike had presented a clear picture of a life lived *his way*.

When Mike explained the time had come to retire and hand the reins of the business over to Chet, he described his son as a young man always willing to learn the next task on the farm. Their firm handshake soon turned into a bear hug between father and son. It was the perfect close to a tender, heartfelt message.

Andrea assumed the applause that followed would lead to an invitation to enjoy the music and buffet waiting for everyone, but when Chet turned and made eye contact with her, Andrea stiffened. She recognized the subtle clues of his unpredictability. *He wouldn't, would he?*

Mike asked his next question into the microphone. "Andrea, would you come on up here and say hello to these fine folks who came out here tonight to help us celebrate?" He gave her an adorable smile that she couldn't refuse with a *no*.

Andrea's hands fell to her chest. "Me?" she

mouthed, hoping he would see how uncomfortable she was with his suggestion. Unlike Mike, taking center stage had the butterflies fluttering in her stomach.

Mike encouraged her. "Come on, now."

She knew there would be no way she'd disappoint Chet's father. Andrea climbed the short flight of stairs and stepped onto the stage.

Mike looked into the eyes of the audience. "Have you heard enough good news for tonight, or could you use a little more?" he asked the crowd.

Hands came together. Hoots and hollers flew from the back of the room. Andrea spotted Chet's brother, Chuck, egging them on, smiling from ear to ear.

It was all the encouragement Mike needed.

He raised his hands and silenced the crowd.

The room quieted.

"It looks like we will have a wedding this Fall." Mike turned from the crowd to face Chet and Andrea. "I'd like to announce my son's engagement to this precious lady, Andrea Lockhart. We couldn't be happier because we love her already."

A long-drawn-out whistle had its effect and re-ignited the crowd in rowdy applause. Chet walked toward the audience with a fist pump.

Adrenaline took a fast track through Andrea's body. The audience's reaction was hokey and sweet, touching that soft spot inside her. All of this was for them – for her and Chet. She felt the sting of unshed tears and couldn't believe this was her life. It was too perfect.

The steady beat of a drum and the strings of a guitar soon filled the room with music. Andrea wasn't sure what was next until Chet offered her his hand. He led her into a twirl across the stage. As the music grew stronger, so did the beating of her heart. The giddiness of a child filled her to the point of feeling lightheaded.

The light pressure of his hand fell to the familiar place on the small of her back. His powerful arms surrounded her as their feet moved with the music. And although it wasn't a dance floor, he led her into a waltz on a wooden-planked stage as if no one else were in the room.

To stay informed on the next book in the series email Christine at cschimpf57@yahoo.com
www.christineschimpf.com
www.goodreads.com/Christine_Schimpf
www.twitter.com/ChrisSchimpf
www.facebook.com/authorchristineschimpf
www.fictionfinder.com